oH

DISCARDED
By
Yuma County Library District

RENEGADE RAMROD

D0732699

RENEGADE RAMROD

LESLIE ERNENWEIN

YUMA COUNTY
LIBRARY DISTRICT
2951 S. 21st Dr. Yuma, AZ 85364
(928) 782-1871
www.yumalibrary.org

WHEELER
CHIVERS

This Large Print edition is published by Wheeler Publishing, Waterville, Maine, USA and by BBC Audiobooks Ltd, Bath, England.
Wheeler Publishing, a part of Gale, Cengage Learning.
Copyright © 1950 by Leslie Ernenwein.
Copyright © 1953 by Leslie Ernenwein in the British Commonwealth.
Copyright © renewed 1978 by the Estate of Leslie Ernenwein.
The moral right of the author has been asserted.

ALL RIGHTS RESERVED
The text of this Large Print edition is unabridged.
Other aspects of the book may vary from the original edition.
Set in 16 pt. Plantin.

LIBRARY OF CONGRESS CATALOGING-IN-PUBLICATION DATA

Ernenwein, Leslie.
   Renegade ramrod / by Leslie Ernenwein. — Large print ed.
     p. cm. — (Wheeler Publishing large print western)
   ISBN-13: 978-1-4104-2946-9 (pbk.)
   ISBN-10: 1-4104-2946-6 (pbk.)
   1. Large type books. I. Title.
   PS3555.R58R44 2010
   813'.54—dc22   2010017706

BRITISH LIBRARY CATALOGUING-IN-PUBLICATION DATA AVAILABLE
Published in 2010 in the U.S. by arrangement with Golden West Literary Agency.
Published in 2010 in the U.K. by arrangement with Golden West Literary Agency.

U.K. Hardcover: 978 1 408 49227 7 (Chivers Large Print)
U.K. Softcover: 978 1 408 49228 4 (Camden Large Print)

Printed in the United States of America
1 2 3 4 5 6 7 14 13 12 11 10

SEP 2 1 2010

RENEGADE RAMROD

5/11

CHAPTER ONE

Afternoon's sharp sunlight slanted over the stone-studded hills west of Tombstone. It fashioned slatted shadow patterns in the O. K. Corral where four saddled horses stood in hipshot patience; it crossed trash-littered alleys and ran down Allen Street where sidewalk loungers watched a painted lady parade her silk and satin finery toward the Can Can Restaurant.

Clay Quantrelle, who stood in front of the restaurant idly prying at his teeth with a toothpick, paid no attention to the approaching woman. He made a tall, lean-shanked shape standing there in the late sunlight; the shabby, range-garbed shape of a drifter. Some past trouble had marked him, giving his gray eyes a questing wariness. His angular, darkly tanned face held a certain refinement of feature which seemed at variance with the scar that deeply rutted his right cheek; yet in this town where toughs were common as mongrel dogs and as numerous, men called him tough.

Tombstone was quiet at this hour, for it was not quite quitting time at the mines. Come sundown a thousand thirsty muckers would stream in from the roundabout shafts — a free-spending horde of homeless toilers wanting to twist the tiger's tail and see the girlies smile. Then the town would stir from its drowsing like a lazy harlot hearing customers at her door; it would absorb them in the Crystal Palace, the Oriental and a dozen lesser mantraps with the effortless ease of a practiced wanton.

Another night of hell on a high stool, Quantrelle thought, not liking his new job as lookout behind Cap Stromberg's poker table at the Crystal Palace Saloon. But a man had to eat, and there'd been no riding jobs when he arrived in town three days ago. A brief, embittered smile altered Quantrelle's long lips. Not a smile, exactly, but more like the fleeting reflection of some past pleasure dimly remembered. There'd been a time when top-hand Texas cowboys were in demand and their rebel yells were heard in every trail town between the Brazos and Dodge City. But those days were gone . . .

The painted lady, a buxom blonde who patronized the Crystal Palace and was sweet on Cap Stromberg, came directly up to Quantrelle, saying, "I've a message for you."

Quantrelle shrugged, disliking this intrusion and showing it in the way he looked at her.

"Cap has a drifter hooked in a head-to-head stud game," the blonde announced. "He wants you to come over, just in case there's trouble."

Quantrelle frowned, thinking: *Bad enough to stay in that stinking place all night, without going to work an hour early.*

"What's the matter?" she demanded poutingly. "Don't you like pretty women enough to give them a smile?"

Quantrelle appraised her bleached curls, her rouged cheeks and the voluptuous swell of a bosom brazenly revealed by the peekaboo cut of her fashionable gown. A "low-and-behold dress", the cowboys called it. The thought came to him that she might have been trapped by circumstances beyond her control — as he had been trapped; that her present profession was merely a means of survival in a rough-and-tumble world. But even so he had an inherent dislike for cat-eyed females who flaunted their womanly wares to lure wages from the pockets of passion-prodded fools. He had seen them ply their ancient trade at Abilene and

Dodge, at Coffeyville and Ellsworth and Wichita. They followed the westward thrust of railroad construction as buzzards had followed gun fights in the Lincoln County War.

It was a deliberate thing, this appraisal — as lingering and calculating as a cattle buyer's tally of beef on the hoof. And as impersonal. Finally he said, "I've seen no pretty women in Tombstone."

Fresh color flamed in the woman's rouged cheeks. She stared at him in momentary disbelief. "Why — you insulting dog!" she shrilled and slashed at his face with a ring-bedecked hand.

Quantrelle did not dodge. Nor docily accept the slap. Instead he lifted an arm with darting swiftness and knocked her hand aside.

"You brute!" she protested hysterically. "You struck me!"

"Then keep your dollar-grabbing hands off brutes," Quantrelle suggested flatly and walked on, paying no heed to inquisitive onlookers until Doc Holliday inquired, "Lovers' quarrel, or do you treat 'em all like that?"

Quantrelle halted. He asked softly — almost whisperingly: "Any business of yours?" and waited, warily poised, until the

10

chalky-cheeked gunman said, "No, I guess not."

Whereupon Quantrelle continued his unhurried walk toward the Crystal Palace.

Belle Langford, who'd once been called the Dixie Songbird and now did her warbling nightly at the Bird Cage Theatre, came out of a millinery shop wearing a little pancake hat with black curled ostrich tips. She smiled at Quantrelle, asking, "How do you like my new hat, Clay?"

He had known her in Abilene when she was a variety stage star — before ten years of trail town trooping had taken the bloom from her cheeks. Looking at her now and seeing what the years had done to her, he thought: *A long time ago.*

"Well," she demanded, "don't you like it?"

"Sure," Quantrelle said and walked on, wanting no revival of a friendship that reminded him of the past. He turned in at the Crystal Palace and was crossing the threshold when a man inside shouted: "I say you second-carded me, Stromberg!"

Quantrelle drew his gun. He stepped quietly into the saloon and saw a man standing half crouched above an overturned chair near the poker table. The man's back was to the doorway, so that Quantrelle couldn't see his face; but he could see the

11

faces of Cap Stromberg and Mike, the fat
bartender who stood just to the right of Cap
with a filled whiskey glass in each hand.

It was a scene wholly familiar to Clay
Quantrelle; a scene witnessed many times
in many places. The pattern seldom varied,
for its ingredients were as elemental as living and dying . . .

"Grab, you goddam cheat!" the stranger
urged, and waggled his cocked gun. "Grab,
or you'll git it cold turkey!"

Stromberg was still seated, his usually
florid face gone pale; his usually loose lips
pulled tight with the pressure of his thinking. Cap was trapped, and he knew it; he
couldn't possibly draw his hideout gun fast
enough to beat the stranger's first shot.
Perspiration greased his flabby cheeks and
dread was a naked thing in his staring eyes
as Quantrelle called sharply: "Drop that
gun!"

There wasn't the slightest suspicion in
Quantrelle's mind that the stranger would
dare disobey that command. No man in his
right senses would choose a shootout at
these odds. But now, seeing the stranger's
shoulders stiffen, Quantrelle thought
amazedly: *He's going to turn!*

The stranger whirled. He fired so franti-
cally fast that the bullet went wide by

inches. Quantrelle's gun blasted at this same instant and it was aimed with a nerveless precision that seemed methodical as two bullets punched twin holes in the stranger's shirt pocket. One of those heavy-calibered slugs ripped through a Durham sack so that tiny flakes of tobacco sifted down as the stranger staggered back against a card table. For a moment he stood there, propped into postured stiffness while he peered at Quantrelle with squint-eyed intensity — as if not seeing his assailant plainly, and wanting to identify him.

Quantrelle was remotely aware of excited voices behind him, but he paid them no heed. His whole attention was focused on the swaying stranger who went down, falling so loosely that his elbows thudded against the floor.

"You got here just in time!" Cap Stromberg exclaimed. He loosed a gusty sigh and wiped his perspiring face with a silk handkerchief. "Thought I was a goner," he admitted frankly. "That galoot was loco, by God — pure loco!"

The bartender handed Stromberg a glass and hastily gulped down the other drink himself. As inquisitive men crowded through the batwings, he announced, "You missed some hair-trigger shootin' if ever I seen it," and peered admiringly at Quantrelle.

Casually, as if this were an old, well-rehearsed performance, Quantrelle poked two empty shells from his gun and refilled the chambers. Then he asked, "What was his name, Cap?"

The gambler shrugged. "Never saw him before he came in and said he wanted to play some table-stake stud."

Cap chuckled, adding, "He sure had a poker sweat up. Tried to win every goddam pot. I never saw a man so set on winning. You'd of thought there was a house rule against him losing."

Quantrelle elbowed through the close-packed crowd of morbid spectators. Why, he wondered, did people like to look at dead men? They were like cattle, attracted by the smell of blood, staring at a pen-slaughtered steer. He stepped over to the bar and poured himself a drink and heard Doc Holliday say, "We better move him into the backroom until Sheriff Behan gets back from Galeyville."

When Quantrelle raised the glass his hand wasn't quite steady. This also was part of the unchanging pattern — the sudden letdown after a shootout, with the backwash of tension having its way. It made him

14

remember Lincoln County; the fresh-dug graves of John Tinstall, Buckshot Roberts and all those others whose blood had stained the red dust redder. Whiskey would melt the cold, clutching knot at the pit of his stomach, but it had never dissolved the sense of awful finality he felt after watching a man die.

Belle Langford came up to the bar, saying, "You look like I feel," and reached for the bottle.

"If I looked like I feel they'd tote me to Boot Hill," Quantrelle muttered.

Belle gulped down a drink, grimacing at its raw burn. "This town gives me the creeps," she complained. "Let's you and me get drunk together, Clay — stinking, dirty, laying down drunk."

"A nice romantic idea," Quantrelle mused and watched two men carry the dead stranger into a backroom. When they came out he said to Belle, "Some other time."

Then he went into the backroom, prodded by a queerly urgent need to know his victim's name. It seemed worse, somehow, to kill a man he didn't know — a man he'd never so much as spoken to until a moment before he shot him.

The body lay sprawled between a row of empty kegs and a broken faro table. The thought came to Quantrelle that this was a fitting place for a corpse, here among discarded things. When life left a man he was empty as those kegs, useless as a broken table. He peered down at the dead man, seeing how the slack-jawed face retained its expression of brutal, ingrained viciousness. Yet he reckoned the stranger's age as being not more than twenty-two or three.

"Young, and tough," Quantrelle muttered, "and old as he'll ever be."

Prompted by an urge he couldn't resist, Quantrelle searched for some clue to the dead rider's identity. The pockets contained nothing of value beyond a few small coins and a knife; no papers of any kind. Quantrelle shrugged, and got up, and was turning to leave when he noticed that the blood-stained shirt was unbuttoned just above the belt buckle.

Believing this might mean there was a moneybelt from which the dead man had extracted cash during the poker game, Quantrelle knelt and found his guess was correct. Quickly unbuckling the canvas belt he observed that three of the flap pockets were open, and empty. The fourth contained a folded sheet of paper on which was written:

Dear Bob:

Please come home at once as Dad needs your help. Unless you come soon and bring some money it may be too late.

Your loving sister, Eve.

A whispering curse crossed Quantrelle's lips. He read the message again, savouring its urgent appeal. A sense of utter solitude slogged through him — an aloneness he had felt many times in the past, but never so devastating as now. Even though this Bob had fired the first shot, Quantrelle found no solace in that fact. No alibi.

The words of the wrinkled letter were like a chant in his ears; like a fear-filled voice calling across a dark canyon. *Unless you come soon and bring some money . . .*

Bob, he thought dismally, had been on his way to answer that summons and stopped off here in a desperate attempt to win the money so urgently needed at home. The irony of it — the sheer futility of attempting to garner a stake from slick-fingered Cap Stromberg — brought a mirthless smile to Quantrelle's lips. As well attempt to extract blood from a stone. Instead of winning, Bob had lost what little money he possessed, and his life with it.

Quantrelle put the letter into his hip

pocket and wondered what town the dead man had been heading toward. His home might have been in Tucson, or Benson, or some ranch in northern Arizona. Quantrelle shrugged, thinking: *He might've been headed for New Mexico, or Texas,* and walked out to the bar.

Cap Stromberg sat at his poker table. "I'm watching the place while Mike eats supper," he said. "Did you find any *dinero* on the chump?"

Quantrelle resented that. "What in hell you think I am — a goddam scavenger?" he demanded. "I searched him to find out who he was."

"Did you?" the gambler asked, idly riffling a deck of cards.

"No, nor any money. You cleaned him out."

"Won a trifle under eighty dollars," Stromberg admitted, and eyed Quantrelle appraisingly. "Perhaps I should split with you for playing the final hand so nice."

Quantrelle shook his head. "I'll take my three days' wages, is all."

"You mean — you're quitting?"

Quantrelle nodded.

"But there's no need for you to run off," Stromberg assured him. "We've got witnesses that you shot in self defense. Mike

18

and I will both swear to that, and it's the truth. That jigger fired first. It was you, or him, and too goddam close for comfort. Johnny Behan will take your word for it, and there'll be no trouble about the shooting. None at all."

Quantrelle thought morosely: *A different kind of trouble, somewhere else.* He said, "I'm leaving town, regardless."

"Aw hell," Cap muttered, frankly disappointed. "You haven't been here long enough to get used to the place. It ain't bad when a man knows his way around. More honey-fussin' women than you can shake a stick at. I'll raise the ante a trifle, if you'll stay on the job."

"I'm drifting," Quantrelle said, and when Stromberg paid him, pocketed the money without counting it.

Leaving the saloon he walked toward the livery where his horse was stabled. This, he reflected, was how he'd felt the day he left Lincoln County right after the battle which ended the Murphy-Chisum feud. Quantrelle frowned, remembering his part in the long war and not liking it. For at the end there'd been no winners. Only survivors. And he was one of them.

In this moment of bitter self judgment Quantrelle saw himself for what he was —

19

an aimless drifter whose trail led always to trouble. Thinking how it had been when he first started out from Texas for a look-see over the hill, Quantrelle marveled at how different life looked at him now. In his youth a man looked ahead, and everything appeared smooth, like mountain slopes brightened by morning sunlight. But later, near sundown, when he got close to the mountain, he discovered the slopes were rough and rocky, with steep ledges and hidden canyons.

At twenty-eight he felt old and washed out, with nothing to show for all the fighting except three days' wages, the clothes on his back and a horse that bore another man's brand. The mountain didn't look smooth to him now; it looked rough.

"Rough as hell," Quantrelle muttered, and remembering the note in his pocket, swore dismally.

A man should be able to make a living without a gun and keep clear of trouble, if he put his mind to it. He could work cattle, or handle a six-horse hitch, or break broncs — any work that didn't call for fighting.

He said, "By God I'm through with the gunsmoke game."

And he meant it, never guessing that the trail would take him to Rincon Basin . . .

■ ■ ■ ■

Clay Quantrelle came to the weather-warped stage station near noon of the fourth day. Seeing this shabby, forlorn place reminded him how threadbare his clothing was, and how few dollars remained in his pockets. He had turned down a riding job yesterday because the ranch looked like a warrior outfit, and now he thought: *I'll have to find something soon.*

Dismounting at the windmill watering trough he let his bay gelding drink its fill. The station hostler came out, walking with an old man's reluctance, and said sourly, "Dished you up a plate of *frijoles.*"

"Gracias," Quantrelle said. He ate the frugal meal in appreciative silence; afterward he asked, "Anyone hiring cow hands, hereabouts?"

The old man glanced speculatively at Quantrelle's gunless hip, noticing the faint pattern a holster had made against the otherwise faded cloth of his riding pants.

"Yeah," he said, "if you've got a gun stowed away in your blanket roll."

Quantrelle shook his head. He shaped a frugal cigarette and lit it and said wearily, "I've had my fill of fighting."

Presently, as he climbed into the saddle, he asked; "How far to the next town?"

"Twenty-seven miles," the hostler said. "Tailholt."

Quantrelle rode on, tilting his hat brim against the sun's brassy glare and smoking the cigarette down until it burned his fingers. It was ironic, he thought, that a man who could earn high wages should be forced to economize on tobacco, and food, and clothing. There was irony too, in the fact that the only work he could find should be gun work. It was enough to make a man discard his dream of peaceful, gracious living.

For a time then, as he rode mile after dusty mile through the desert's scorching heat, Quantrelle's dismal thoughts were like bickering companions nagging at his mind, clawing at the thin fabric of his determination. What good was it for a man to strive against the strong tide of circumstance? Dame fortune had stacked the cards at the start and a man had to play them the way they were dealt. Or so it seemed.

Afterward he rimmed a long divide and rode toward the town of Tailholt, observing how insignificant it seemed against the vast sweep of brush-blotched slopes and timbered hills beyond it. Good country, he thought, big country. And because of what lay behind him, he said with sober hopefulness, "A place to start over again."

Allowing the bay to set its own pace, Quantrelle wondered if the animal's brand would be recognized as John Chisum's — and supposed it would be. His own private horse, crippled by a bullet, had been left in Chisum's corral the day he left New Mexico.

Presently, as Quantrelle followed the stageroad into a dry wash, he came upon the remains of a burned freight wagon. Its cargo of spooled barb wire made a flame-blackened mound above charred embers and metal braces. Contemplating this and seeing that other wagons had detoured around the wreckage, Quantrelle wondered why none of them had picked up the blackened wire. Then, seeing how completely the fire had consumed even the hickory spokes and singletrees, he understood that the flames had taken the temper from the barbed wire, rendering it worthless.

"Must've been plenty hot," Quantrelle reflected and went on, having no more than a drifter's mild interest in the mishap.

Afterward, as he rode into Tailholt, a whimsical smile creased Quantrelle's dust-peppered face. The town was like a peaceful oasis in the desert. Gnarled mesquites shaded pleasant homes in the residential section, and the delicate shadow patterns of ancient pepper trees dappled the plaza's wide dust. Two saddled horses dozed at the Belvedere Saloon's gnawed hitch rack; a cowboy chatted with a young woman on the Mercantile stoop, and farther down the street an old man sat whittling in the wide doorway of Pardee's Livery.

"A real quiet town," Quantrelle mused, liking it at once.

The young woman on the Mercantile stoop laughed, that lilting sound reminding Quantrelle how long a time it had been since he'd heard a respectable woman laugh. Her face was turned, giving him a profile view of smooth contours that were in graceful harmony with her sweet-toned voice and with the dusky curls clustered at the nape of her neck.

Comparing her with Tombstone's painted ladies, Quantrelle thought: *A real beauty,* and had an urgent desire to wait here until she turned toward him so that he might see her face fully. But he shrugged off the impulse; quartering toward the livery stable he took care to ride around a sleeping dog so as not to disturb it. Tailholt, he decided, would be a fine place to rest for a few days; to eat and sleep and forget the past. As simple as that it seemed to him; just food and lodging, and a chance to forget.

Thus Clay Quantrelle rode toward Pardee's Livery in the relaxed fashion of a man at peace with the world. It didn't occur to Quantrelle that men would invariably judge him to be older than his twenty-eight years, nor that the puckered scar that whitely dimpled his right cheek, gave his face a devil-be-damned toughness that was in direct contrast to his new code of conduct. He thought only of the quiet, sun-lit town and was content.

Dismounting in front of the livery Quantrelle nodded to the tobacco-chewing proprietor who sat on a bench at one side of the barn's wide doorway. Pardee glanced speculatively at the bay's brand and said, "Lincoln County."

The way he spoke those two words, showing neither censure nor satisfaction, told Quantrelle that forgetting the past might not be so simple. Half the folks in Tailholt would know within the hour that he was riding a Chisum branded horse. Some of them not knowing what Billy the Kid looked like, might take him for the bucktoothed killer the newspapers had so widely publicized. But even so, Quantrelle had no premonition of trouble. Unsaddling the bay he turned the tired horse over to Pardee, saying, "A full measure of grain and all the hay he'll eat."

The liveryman nodded and led the horse into a stall. Quantrelle untied his blanket roll and took out a soiled duffel sack which contained his few personal belongings. He thought: *I'll shave off these whiskers and eat supper in style at the hotel,* and wondered if the dark-haired young woman would also patronize the hotel dining room. The realization that he was that much interested in a woman, startled him. Must be the altitude, he thought; or the fact he hadn't seen a female for a few days.

Pardee asked, "Goin' to stay in town for a spell?"

"A day or so," Quantrelle said. He gave Main Street a brief appraisal, noting the arrangement of its business establishments, and added, "Looks real peaceable."

"So does dynamite," Pardee said in a cynical, complaining voice, "until it explodes."

Quantrelle eyed him wonderingly. There was no friendliness in the man's pudgy, whisker-stubbled face, nor in his faded blue eyes. Yet he seemed anxious to talk. "You expecting it to explode?" Quantrelle asked.

Pardee nodded, squirting an amber dollop of tobacco juice into the dust.

"What's the trouble?" Quantrelle inquired.

"What's always the trouble in cow country," Pardee muttered crankily. "Grass and water and barb wire."

He pointed a finger at a blond, broad-shouldered cowboy on the Mercantile stoop and said, "That's Hal Barton. He organized the Rincon Basin Pool which is feudin' with Pat Tanner's Big T."

"Pat Tanner?" Quantrelle demanded, urgently interested now. "Apache Pat Tanner who drove a trail herd to Ellsworth?"

Pardee nodded, asked, "You know him?"

"Yeah," Quantrelle mused. A reflective smile briefly eased his long lips. Then, as the full significance of Pardee's report dawned on him, a thoughtful frown replaced the smile. This country had looked good — so big and quiet — but the knowledge that Pat Tanner was in trouble here altered the picture completely. For Clay Quantrelle owed Tanner the biggest debt a man could owe anyone — his life.

He thought: *Dame Fortune has cold-decked me again.* The trifling old bawd was still dealing the cards. It was ironic that he should come seeking peace in a country where Apache Pat Tanner was involved in range war. A hellish joke on a man wanting to make a fresh, clean start. Wanting to forget the smoky past . . .

"How soon you figure the fighting will start?" Quantrelle inquired.

"Already started," Pardee said. He took out a plug of tobacco, bit off a fresh chew and tongued it far up in his left cheek. Then he said, "The Pool put up a drift fence betwixt Big T and the range they claimed was theirs. Big T pulled it down, and when the Pool tried to bring in more barb wire the freight wagon was held up."

"So that's why the wagon was burned," Quantrelle mused. "Did Big T riders do the job?"

"It happened after dark, so the driver couldn't see their faces," Pardee reported. "But who the hell else would of done it?"

The same old story, Quantrelle thought. Night riders rimming the ridges, gut-shot horses screaming out their agony; wounded men whimpering in the dismal dawn. No matter how the gunsmoke game got started it always settled into the same sorry pattern. It would be like Lincoln County, and the blood-spattered Ruidoso. Only the names and the brands were different . . .

"Is the Pool strong enough to whip Tanner's outfit?" Quantrelle asked.

Instead of answering, Pardee gestured toward the big cowboy who had left the

28

Mercantile stoop and was now coming this way. "Ask Barton," he suggested. "Hal knows all the answers. Leastwise most folks around here seem to think he does."

Hal Barton wore the typical garb of a working cow-puncher, but he walked in the chesty, strutting fashion of an actor crossing a stage. *All swelled up with self importance,* Quantrelle thought, watching him cross the sidewalk.

Barton peered sharply at Quantrelle's face, not speaking while his appraisal shifted to the duffel sack and remained there momentarily, as if noting the gungear that bulged one side of the sack. Then he asked, "Looking for a job?"

Quantrelle ignored the question while he returned the inspection, glance for glance. Barton looked to be in his late twenties — a blocky, bland-faced man with yellow hair and hooded eyes. There was a brash glint in his tawny eyes now, and an arrogance in the way he asked, "Well, do you, or don't you?"

"I guess not," Quantrelle said civilly.

Barton peered at Quantrelle's gunless hip, giving the holster-shaped pattern a deliberate consideration. "I could use a good man," he announced.

"Not interested," Quantrelle said. "I'm just passing through."

"How far through?" Barton asked bluntly.

A long established custom of meeting toughness with toughness prompted Quantrelle to ask, "Any of your business?"

"Yes," Barton said without hesitation. "I'm president of the Rincon Basin Pool. When strangers ride into this country I want to know where they're going."

"So?" Quantrelle mused. Here, he decided, was a man who'd got too big for his britches. Remembering that Barton had been talking to a lovely young woman on the Mercantile stoop, Quantrelle thought: *Thinks he's the main stud.* Either that, or he was looking for a fight. But why in hell should Barton want to pick a quarrel? What possible gain could there be in it for him, or for the Pool he represented? It didn't make sense.

"How far through you riding?" Barton demanded.

This was Lincoln County all over again. The same brutal pressure against neutrality; the same sharp-eyed suspicion and wary probing. A man couldn't be a free individual. He had to belong to one side or the other, regardless of what his personal feelings were. A few minutes ago Tailholt had seemed like an oasis — a safe sanctuary for trail-weary travelers. Now the smell of trouble was like the stink of gunsmoke tainting the air of the sunlit street.

"How far you going?" Barton persisted.

Quantrelle ignored that arrogance, and shrugged off the resentment it kindled. A man could keep out of trouble only if he refused to accept trouble. He grinned, making an open-palmed gesture with his right hand and asked, "How far does a drifter know how far he'll ride?"

"So you're just another tramp on horseback," Barton scoffed.

The deliberate maliciousness of it clawed at Quantrelle's patience. For a moment he teetered on the thin edge of letting temper have its way with him. But some remnant of stubborn resolve held him back. Tucking the duffel sack under one arm he shaped a cigarette and lit it, allowing smoke to filter leisurely from his nostrils before saying, "You have a right to your opinion."

That seemed to annoy Hal Barton. He exclaimed, "A coward also, by God!"

Joe Pardee, who'd stood silent until now, said nervously, "He's ridin' a Chisum branded horse, Hal."

"I didn't ask you anything," Barton snapped, not glancing at the livery man. Then he said to Quantrelle, "Just a shiftless, greasy-sack drifter."

Quantrelle felt embarrassment flush his cheeks. He felt anger beat its way through his veins, the pressure of it so strong that it thudded in his temples. He eyed Barton narrowly, endeavoring to guess a reasonable explanation for such belligerence. The Pool boss wasn't drunk, nor did he seem overly wrathful. There was an expression in his eyes now that Quantrelle couldn't identify, but it didn't look like anger.

"Whatever you say," Quantrelle agreed. He tossed his cigarette into the street, and was like that — with his right arm extended — when Barton hit him.

Caught utterly unprepared and off balance, Quantrelle floundered sideways. He collided with Pardee's low, oak bench which cut his feet from under him so that he fell backward, striking his head against the plank doorframe.

"What the hell!" Joe Pardee blurted in bug-eyed astonishment. He contemplated Quantrelle's motionless form, then peered at Barton, demanding, "Why'd you hit him?"

Barton shrugged, said, "Douse the dirty son with water," and walked on along the street.

A hardware drummer, seeing all this from the Empire Hotel veranda, hurried across the street. And John Tuck, wearing a black patch over his left eye, came from his blacksmith shop next door, asking, "Why did Hal hit him?"

"Damned if I know," Pardee muttered and sluiced a full bucket of water into Quantrelle's face. "Never saw the beat of it. Never knowed Hal Barton to act so goddam mean."

Clay Quantrelle propped himself up on his elbows. He shook his head in dazed wonderment. He became aware of the stable's rank odor, and a wetness that blurred his vision. He rubbed his eyes and when they focused properly, looked up at Pardee. "What," he asked, "did Barton hit me with?"

"His fist," Joe reported. "But that wasn't what put out your lights. You fell over the bench and hit the doorframe with your noggin."

Quantrelle got up, retrieved his battered hat and put it on.

The one-eyed blacksmith asked, "You feel all right, stranger?"

Quantrelle nodded, and fingered the lump on the back of his head, just above his right ear.

"Barton plays a trifle rough," he observed, revealing no anger. But resentment pounded a twin beat to the throb of his aching head and there was in him now a sense of outrage unlike anything he'd ever known — a new and shameful sense of persecution. For the first time in his life Clay Quantrelle had docily accepted abuse. An odd feeling. And the cause of it seemed equally odd. How had Barton guessed that a total stranger would refuse to fight? The Pool boss, he supposed, wouldn't have been so free with his fists against an armed man. But even so, Barton's belligerence didn't make sense.

"You took a lot off Hal," Joe Pardee said, plainly puzzled. "A God awful lot, considerin'."

"Considering what?" Quantrelle asked sharply.

"Well, considerin' that you don't exactly look like no Gentle Annie, and ridin' a Chisum branded horse, and all."

A self-mocking smile quirked Quantrelle's lips. The liveryman couldn't understand such meekness. He probably tallied it for cowardice, the same as Barton. Well, they'd know different, directly. He had given the peace-at-any-price proposition a fair trial and it hadn't worked. So thinking, Quantrelle opened the duffel sack, took out his gungear and strapped it on.

"Changed your mind?" Pardee asked slyly.

Ignoring the question and paying no heed to the little group of curious bystanders, Quantrelle walked out to the street. But he couldn't help hearing the one-eyed blacksmith predict, "There goes trouble on the hoof if ever I saw it!" And Joe Pardee said, "I still can't figger out why he let Barton rawhide him like that. You'd of thought he was a slick-eared button scairt of his own shadow."

Quantrelle crossed the plaza in leisurely fashion. But his thoughts weren't leisurely; they were racing ahead to the moment when he would face Barton again. There was in him now a queerly contrasting mixture of anticipation and regret — a cross pull of anger-prodded eagerness and dismal frustration. For the first time in his life he had attempted to sidestep trouble, refusing to accept it. And had been knocked down for his meekness.

From out of his boyhood came the memory of a mother's counsel to a son who was often in bloody-nosed brawls with his playmates; "It takes two to make a fight, Clay. Always remember that."

Well, it hadn't taken two this time. Hal Barton had forced the fight and finished it, all by himself . . .

Quantrelle's sun-puckered eyes were

35

warily watchful as he crossed Main Street and went up the hotel veranda steps. A man couldn't take what he had taken without fighting back. There was a limit to the cheek-turning deal, and he had passed it. The world was a damned dog-eat-dog affair, anyway. He'd been a witless fool to think it was otherwise.

Now that he was armed, Quantrelle wondered if Barton would draw a gun against him; or if the second deal would be a fist fight. The Pool boss, he judged, outweighed him by ten or fifteen pounds, but that wasn't overly important. It wasn't how much a man weighed, that counted; it was how he handled himself. Remembering the rough-and-tumble brawls he'd been in at one time or another, Quantrelle grinned confidently.

He thought: *I'll be ready for him this time, whichever way it goes,* and at this moment collided with a woman in the hotel doorway — the dusky-haired young woman who'd stood with Hal Barton on the Mercantile stoop.

The force of impact jolted her off balance so that she grasped him with both arms to keep from falling. In this moment of confusion, as they clung to each other in a mutual need for support, it was as if they were locked in passionate embrace. Her body made a definite pressure against him — an intimate, cushioning pressure that was hugely pleasing.

As if sharing this sense of intimacy and astonished by it, she drew away. Her face, which at the moment of collision had gone pale, was flushed now, her blue eyes were bright with excitement — or anger.

Quantrelle stepped aside, saying, "Beg pardon, ma'am."

She put her slim fingers to tucking back a lock of tumbled hair. She said, "I guess it was as much my fault as yours."

And then she smiled, revealing the full loveliness her profile had indicated — an oval, high-cheeked face that held a fragile delicacy made more pronounced by long black eyelashes. Yet her straight nose flared gently at the nostrils when she smiled and her lips were full and moist and expressive. The lips of a generous and passionate woman.

Again, as he had when he first saw her, Quantrelle thought: *A real beauty,* and was wholly confused by the attraction she held for him. Remembering his manners, he took off his hat and said, "Name of Quantrelle — Clay Quantrelle."

Her smile, which had faded under his

lingering appraisal, returned to dimple her smooth cheeks. She said, "I'm Eve Chalice, and I don't make a practice of rushing blindly into men's arms."

Quantrelle grinned, liking the composed and low-toned quality of her voice. Liking also the warm glowing of her eyes. "I'm glad it happened," he admitted frankly.

For a moment, as she smiled up at him with comradely amusement, Quantrelle thought she was going to admit a kindred pleasure. He even hoped she might share some part of the magnetic attraction she held for him; but she laughed softly and went on out to the veranda without speaking again.

Quantrelle watched her go down the steps, seeing how gracefully she moved as she crossed the sunlit plaza, holding her skirt out of the dust. He wished that she would glance back at him, for he wanted another look at her face; and knew she wouldn't. Proper young women didn't play the coquette role in a public place; that was for females hunting a man. The trifling trollops who played up to gunsmoke drifters.

"Eve Chalice," he mused, liking the sound of it and deciding that the name fitted her exactly, being unusually nice. He wondered if he'd see her again before he left town, and hoped he would, and was astonished that he should feel this way about a woman he hadn't seen an hour ago. It occurred to him now that he was gawking at her like a skirt-chasing dude, whereupon he turned into the hotel lobby and asked for a front room.

Afterward, shaving in front of a fly-specked mirror, Quantrelle remembered what Joe Pardee had said about the feud between Big T and the Pool. It would be like Pat Tanner to buck a half dozen outfits. That was old Apache Pat's way. The odds made no difference to Tanner if he thought he was right. Thinking back to the promise he'd once made, Quantrelle repeated it slowly, using the exact words as he remembered them: "If you ever need a helping hand I'll come running."

Quantrelle frowned into the mirror. The lather had been scraped from his right cheek exposing the puckered scar which now reminded him of the night Pat Tanner had saved his life at Ellsworth. Quantrelle grimaced, recalling the raw wildness of that turbulent trail town and his brief part in it . . .

"A long time ago," he reflected, and counting the years, was astonished that it was less than five. He had won a lot of money that night; more money than he'd ever possessed before — or since. So much money that the percentage of girls had swarmed around him like flies at a sorghum keg. Quantrelle smiled, remembering how eagerly the swivel-rumped teasers had tempted him with their kiss-pouted lips and caressing hands; how they'd used all their tricks of practiced revealment and sensuous appeal. They'd acted itchy as mares in heat — like they were panting for the privilege of being served by a stud. But he had laughed at the cat-eyed lot of them, and at the slick tinhorns who'd invited him to try his luck at other games.

"This is the stake I've been waiting for," he had told them. "The stake that's going to build me the biggest little cow outfit in Texas."

He'd been the big mogul then. And felt high as a windmill . . .

But ten minutes later he'd been robbed by two men who slugged him as he passed a dark alley on his way out of Nauchville, that infamous Gomorrah of saloons and sporting houses at the east end of Ellsworth. He'd been almost unconscious when they took his money, yet he heard one man speak and recognized his voice. Or thought he did. A gambler called Scarface Shambrun.

Thinking back to that night now, Quantrelle couldn't recall the name of the saloon where he'd found Shambrun and accused him of the holdup. But he vividly remembered every other detail: how Scarface had drawn and fired before his own gun was free of holster — how that first bullet had gouged his cheek and the second slug had missed him only because a tough old trail driver named Apache Pat Tanner had clouted Shambrun's right wrist with a quart bottle.

As close as that, it had been, with Apache Pat representing the difference between living and dying for a confused young Texan . . .

Tanner had his gun out and fully cocked when he stepped up beside Quantrelle. He'd loosed a loud rebel yell, then laughed at Scarface Shambrun and all the other riff-raff, saying, "I ain't killed me a flea-bitten, burr-tailed coyote for a week and I'm just honin' for the chance!"

There'd been a hushed and lingering interval when half a dozen trail-town toughs wavered on the thin edge of drawing; a seemingly endless interval while Clay Quantrelle had gripped his gun in sweat-greased fingers and a blonde trollop at the bar giggled hysterically. But Pat Tanner wasn't sweating. He was chuckling, taunting them to try their luck.

"Grab your goddam guns and we'll have us a time — Texas style!" he shouted gleefully. "Come one at a time, or all together!"

Never in all the years of his wandering, had Quantrelle seen the like of it. For Tanner wasn't drunk. The old rannyhan may have downed a dozen drinks during the evening, but he wasn't drunk.

"What the hell you waitin' on?" he'd asked them. "Ain't there no men in this stinkin' place at all?"

And because he so surely meant it, neither Scarface Shambrun nor any of his hardcase companions had accepted that brazen challenge . . .

A whimsical smile creased Quantrelle's freshly shaved face as he put away the razor. He hadn't got his money back, but that didn't seem important after Shambrun's fast draw — after that first bullet had gouged his cheek. He'd been glad to leave Nauchville alive, with Apache Pat Tanner walking beside him. So glad that when they parted at the Grand Central bar an hour later he'd said, "If you ever need a helping hand I'll come running."

And now, according to Joe Pardee, Tanner needed a helping hand.

Quantrelle peered down at the plaza, observing that Joe Pardee stood on the Belvedere Saloon stoop talking to three men. Hal Barton wasn't there, and now one of the men, a saddle-warped oldster with a down-swirling mustache, limped along the street to Matabelle's Millinery where Eve Chalice stepped out to meet him. Her father, Quantrelle guessed, and noticed that she toted a hat box as she accompanied him toward the livery stable. Presently, as they drove away from the barn in a buckboard, it occurred to him that Chalice probably belonged to the Pool.

That supposition sobered him. Getting into another range war would be bad enough, but if keeping his promise to Tanner meant fighting against Eve Chalice's father . . .

He was still standing at the window when a ranch wagon came out of the Mercantile yard, piled high with provisions. Two riders flanked the wagon, six-guns at their hips and carbines in saddle scabbards.

"An armed escort," Quantrelle mused, and noticed a Big T brand on the horse nearest him. Then, as he turned from the window, he saw the door of his room swing open and Hal Barton stepped inside.

Quantrelle froze, urgently aware that his

gungear was draped over a chair six feet away. Barton's gun was holstered and his right hand was close to it, but the Pool boss didn't look belligerent now. He looked friendly.

"I'm sorry you fell so hard," Barton said. "If you hadn't tripped you could've gone down without hurting yourself at all."

Quantrelle nodded agreement, concealing the astonishment that rifled through him. What was Barton talking about? And why was he smiling in such congenial fashion? The Pool boss hadn't made sense at the livery; now he sounded downright loco.

Barton reached into his pants pocket, brought out two double-eagles and offered them to Quantrelle, saying, "Here's the knockdown payoff as promised."

Then, while Quantrelle accepted the money, Barton said, "Wyatt told me I'd recognize you by the scar on your face, but I thought he said it was on your left cheek."

Quantrelle fingered the scar, said, "Maybe he got mixed up," and wondered if the Wyatt mentioned was Wyatt Earp at Tombstone. And what this was all about . . .

"You sure picked out a classy name," Barton chided, "considering the one you usually go by."

"Yeah," Quantrelle agreed, understanding

44

now that this was a case of mistaken identity. Barton thought he was someone else — someone he'd expected. That deal at the liverystable had been framed up in advance. But for what purpose? Was it for Joe Pardee's benefit, or someone else's?

Quantrelle said, "Wyatt didn't go into details, much. What's the setup here?"

"It's simple, and practically fool-proof," Barton bragged. He took out a cigar and bit off its end and said, "There never was a setup like it, friend."

Watching him light the cigar and puff it to even burning, Quantrelle revised his first opinion of Barton. The man was now the very personification of graciousness, and close to being handsome, for the change in his manner altered his whole appearance. *A born actor,* Quantrelle reflected, and understood that he was dealing with a complex and thoroughly clever rascal . . .

"I want a man of my own at Tanner's ranch to keep me posted on what's going on," Barton explained. "And to give Ike Gallatin a hand when the showdown comes. Ike says Tanner is so suspicious he might not hire somebody that came to him cold. But this way, with you and me having trouble, Tanner is sure to put you on the payroll. He would hire the devil himself if

45

he thought the devil disliked me."

"So that's why the knockdown was framed," Quantrelle thought aloud. "I was wondering what it was for."

Then he asked, "Who's this Ike Gallatin you're talking about?"

"Tanner's foreman," Barton said, smiling in a thoroughly satisfied way. "That's why the deal is fool-proof. Ike has to stick pretty close to the ranch, but being ramrod, he can fix it so you can get away whenever there's a message for me. There's going to be some big doings in this country, friend — some real big doings, and I'm getting set to be on the winning end."

"So that's how it is," Quantrelle reflected, marveling at this blonde man's frankness. Barton, he decided, was so sure of winning that he could afford to be free with his predictions.

"You ever hear of a better rigged proposition?" Barton asked smilingly.

"No," Quantrelle admitted. "I never did."

He idly juggled the two golden pieces in his left hand. This, he thought, was about as double-crossing a deal as he had ever known. A combine of small ranchers seldom went in for such elaborate and underhanded strategy. Wanting to obtain the complete picture, he risked another direct question, asking, "What's in it for me? Wyatt said it was a big deal — not just gun wages."

"It is big," Barton bragged. "So big it'll change things all around in Rincon Basin, if we win. And I don't see how in hell we can miss winning. The whole setup will be changed."

"How?"

Barton stuck his thumbs behind his belt and teetered slowly back and forth on his heels. His bland smile remained, but his amber-flecked eyes turned cold and brittle as he said, "The deal is big enough to pay you a thousand dollar bonus. Isn't that all you need to know?"

And when Quantrelle remained silent, Barton demanded, "Don't that sound big enough?"

"Yeah," Quantrelle muttered, "but a trifle too dirty."

Then he pitched forward, hitting Barton so quickly that his hands were only half raised; so hard that Barton was already collapsing when the second blow caught him just below the left ear. The Pool boss grunted once on his way down, then spraddled out full length and lay motionless.

Quantrelle peered down at him, thinly smiling. "That evens the score," he said, rubbing his bruised knuckles on a pants leg.

Then he bent over Barton's blocky, loose-featured face and placed a goldpiece on either eye. After which he buckled on his gungear and went out of the room, closing the door behind him.

CHAPTER TWO

The hotel diningroom was deserted save for one waitress who sat at a rear table reading a newspaper. Quantrelle chose a table against the east wall which gave him a view of the stairway. Barton, he suspected, would be a trifle on the prod when he came down those stairs . . .

The waitress came over and took his order of a T-bone steak, fried potatoes, apple pie and coffee. It was a better meal than he had ordered since leaving Tombstone and he thought: *I'm eating high off the hog tonight.*

A middle-aged man with a star on his vest came into the diningroom. He moved, Quantrelle thought, like a man seldom sober — as if walking straight was a chore that demanded strict attention. He started to take a table near the doorway, then peered at Quantrelle and crossed the room, asking, "Are you the stranger that had the fuss with Hal Barton?"

Quantrelle nodded, and smiled a little, thinking of what had happened upstairs. Joe Pardee hadn't mentioned the fact that there was a sheriff in Tailholt; now Quantrelle wondered where he stood in the Big T-Pool feud. Smack dab in the middle, probably.

"I'm George Weaver," the sheriff said. "Mind if I sit down here?"

"Not at all," Quantrelle said graciously, contemplating this man's spongy, red-veined face and the dull meekness of his eyes. A boozer, he decided, and tallied Weaver as a disillusioned man who drank to forget his troubles. Every town had them; they were, he reasoned, an inevitable by-product of progress. The larger a town grew the more drunks it produced.

"From what I hear, Hal Barton treated you a trifle rough," Sheriff Weaver suggested.

Quantrelle nodded. "A trifle," he agreed.

The waitress, also middle-aged but retaining a quality of girlish charm, brought his order. Then she asked, "The usual, George?"

"Yes, Mae," Weaver said, and now Quantrelle was aware of some definite tension between them. They were, he thought, like old and established enemies being polite to each other. Or old friends who'd had a falling out . . .

When Mae departed, the sheriff said regretfully, "There was a time when Mae Bowen was willin' to become Mrs. Weaver, but this damn star got in the way."

"So?" Quantrelle prompted.

Weaver fiddled with his fork, as if wanting to talk and not knowing exactly how to go about it. Finally he asked, "You fixin' to file an assault charge agin Barton?"

Quantrelle shook his head, and went on with his eating.

"I hear you're from Lincoln County," Weaver said.

Quantrelle neither acknowledged nor denied that supposition. He asked, "Make any difference where a man is from?"

"Not a bit," Weaver assured. "I just thought you might be lookin' for a job. If you are, I think you might find one at Big T, considerin' what happened between you and Hal Barton. His Pool is feudin' with Big T."

That surprised Quantrelle. Cow country lawmen seldom took such obvious sides in a range feud, with total strangers. Most of them preferred to act neutral and let the trouble run its course, knowing they couldn't stop it. But Weaver was practically announcing that he wanted Pat Tanner to win against the Pool. Which seemed odd, especially from so meek and fumbling a man.

"Are you backing Big T?" Quantrelle asked.

A sheepish smile loosened Weaver's lips. "Not exactly," he explained. "It's — well, the other way around. Big T got me elected to office."

And Mae doesn't like it, Quantrelle guessed. Keeping the lower stairway on the rim of his vision, he asked, "How about the rest of this town? Are most folks against Pat Tanner?"

"They are now, since the wagonload of wire was burned. Up to then it was just the opposite, most people favorin' Apache Pat against Barton, who's a Johnny-come-lately in Rincon Basin. Pat was here before any of 'em. His Big T was the first brand and he had to fight Apaches to protect it. But that wire burnin' deal soured folks on Pat, even though he swears his crew didn't do it. The Pool had just about broke themselves buyin' that wire. Two-three of 'em had to mortgage their places with a Tucson bank. And they stand to lose 'em if the Pool don't win real soon."

Mae brought Weaver's meal, scarcely glancing at him as she served it. The sheriff,

Quantrelle observed, watched her in the shy, troubled fashion of a man eyeing a prize eagerly desired and hopelessly beyond obtaining. The way he himself might one day look at Eve Chalice . . . *Eve!*

Until this momennt the name hadn't registered on him. Now its significance hurtled through him with an awful clarity. The note he'd taken from a dead man's moneybelt had been signed Eve — *Your loving sister, Eve!*

Forcing his voice to a casual tone, Quantrelle asked, "Does Chalice have a son?"

"Yes, but he's off sashayin' around Texas some place," Weaver reported. "Young Bob was born fiddle-footed. Guess he takes after his mammy, who was a variety show dancer until shc married Jim Chalice. She died two years ago, God bless her poor soul. Never could get used to ranch livin'."

Quantrelle went through the motions of eating his pie. But it was tasteless. Back there in Tombstone he had wanted to know the name of the man he'd killed. Well, he knew it now. Bob Chalice. And he knew the sister who'd pleaded for him to come home. A sighing curse slid from Quantrelle's lips. Dame Fortune, he thought dismally, had never done a better job of stacking the deck.

"Joe Pardee says you used to know Pat Tanner," the sheriff said. "Joe is a real fine feller, when you git to know him. He thought you might be figgerin' to sign on with Apache Pat."

Quantrelle put his fingers to shaping a cigarette. Without knowing it, this boozy sheriff had hit the bulls-eye — the big question that had to be answered. The question that Clay Quantrelle couldn't avoid answering to himself. On the one side was his forlorn hope for peaceful living, and the urgent attraction Eve Chalice held for him. On the other side was a debt and a promise that could be evaded by riding on out of Rincon Basin, but never be forgotten. No man could ride away from himself, nor could he ride far enough to forget that he had deliberately avoided keeping a solemn promise.

"You reckon Apache Pat needs help?" he asked, hoping for a negative answer and knowing how useless that hope was.

"Yes," Weaver said without hesitation. "He sure as hell does."

"How far is Big T from town?"

"About seventeen miles, almost due west," Weaver said. "Follow the stageroad until you pass a mailbox that's marked with a Cross Crescent. That's Jim Chalice's place. Then take the north road at the forks just beyond, and you'll end up at Big T."

"How much of a crew does Pat have?"

"Not much, since the big drought whittled him down," Weaver said, and tallied the riders aloud: "There's Ike Gallatin, his ramrod, Red Parmalee, Kid Calhoun, Jim Jeddy and a Mex called Sonora. That makes five, not countin' Gramp Pettigrue, who's six years older than God."

"Nor you," Quantrelle said slyly.

Weaver didn't like that and showed it in the frown that tightened his face. "I'm not on Tanner's payroll and never have been, since I took this job," he announced. "Regardless of what folks think, that's the truth!"

Quantrelle grinned, said, "I believe you," and meant it. "A man gets tangled up with friendship, sometimes — and pays a price for it."

"A God-awful price," Weaver agreed sighingly.

Quantrelle heard footsteps on the stairs. He kept watching, seeing a man's boots descend, and was almost certain they belonged to Hal Barton. He wondered what the Pool boss would do when he saw him here with Weaver. Probably nothing. But Barton was wholly unpredictable; he might demand a showdown fist fight, here and now.

Then, as the man's upper body came into view, Quantrelle saw that it was the one-eyed blacksmith, coming down for supper. Barton, he thought, must be waiting for him upstairs. With a gun, perhaps.

Finished with his meal, Quantrelle got up, and Weaver asked, "You goin' to hire on with Tanner, sure enough?"

Quantrelle nodded, whereupon the sheriff said in a pleased way, "Pat will need every gun he can git, to my way of thinkin'." He glanced at Quantrelle's low-slung holster, adding, "I'm sure pleased you're goin' to side him."

A cynical smile quirked Quantrelle's lips. Gunsmoke, he guessed, had a way of tainting a man, so that total strangers could look at him and know what he was. Or what he had been.

"You goin' out to Big T tonight?" Weaver asked.

"Tomorrow," Quantrelle said and leaving the diningroom, went slowly upstairs, not sure of what he would find. The hallway was dimly lighted by one bracket lamp. Moving quietly so he came to the closed door of the room. Barton, he felt sure, hadn't hit his head on anything when he fell, and those two blows shouldn't have paralyzed him for this length of time. Yet he was equally sure that the Pool boss hadn't come down the stairs.

Quantrelle drew his gun, guessing that Barton might be inside and wanting a shootout. He listened for a long moment, hearing no sound. Then he turned the knob, pushed the door wide open and stepped aside. The room was empty.

It occurred to Quantrelle now that Barton, feeling none too well after being knocked out, had chosen to use a back stairway to make his exit. Going into the room and closing the door he proceeded to change the furniture around so that the bed would be in a different position. Just in case Barton decided to send a couple of slugs through the door later on . . .

Dog tired, and drowsy from the big meal, Quantrelle undressed and got into bed. This, he supposed, would be his last free night as a footloose drifter. No telling how long the range war would last, nor how tough it would become. There'd be long nights asaddle, and many dismal dawns. There'd be cursing men leaving bloodstains on the brush. All this was familiar to him, like a part in an old and unchanging stage play. There had been a time when he took it as a matter of course — a price to pay for the privilege of being his own man. But that bloody mess in Lincoln County had cured him, and the Tombstone shooting had turned him sick inside. Now, because Eve Chalice had walked into his arms, this deal would be even worse.

Quantrelle was thinking about that, and about the necessity of exposing Ike Gallatin, when he finally went to sleep.

George Weaver was drunk. Not staggering drunk but just pleasantly, swaying drunk. He left the Belvedere Saloon by its rear door and moved slowly along the back alley, wanting to have a talk with Joe Pardee. Joe was a real friend. But not his best friend. Whiskey was a man's best friend. It made him forget he'd almost had himself a wife — the warmest, sweet-loving woman a man ever met. Whiskey gave him a glow inside, it made him feel ten feet tall if he drank enough. And proud, like he'd used to be. It made him feel like holding up his head and maybe strutting a trifle, the way a sheriff should.

By force of long habit, Weaver avoided collision with trash barrels and rubbish piles that littered the dark alley. He had made this night journey to Pardee's barn many times during the past few weeks, choosing the route so there'd be no chance of Mae seeing him. Mae disliked whiskey something awful. She called it a devil's brew and scorned any man who drank it.

That, George thought, was the funny part of it. He hadn't been a boozer until Mae quit him cold. Up until then he'd hardly touched the stuff, except on special occasions. So it was really Mae who'd turned him into a drinker. Which seemed uncommon odd, when you considered how she hated booze.

Coming to the corral behind the livery, Weaver crawled through the fence and walked over a manure pile to the barn's rear doorway. There was something real comfortable about a livery stable, he thought. It had a good smell of horses and harness and liniment. Reminded him of his boyhood, when he'd earned his first dollar cleaning stalls for his father. "Ain't nothin' more healthy than horse manure for a man," his father had told him.

A lighted lantern hung at one side of the front entrance, casting a cheerful ray down the long runway between two rows of stalls. Weaver spoke quietly to horses on either side of him and was careful to keep an approximately straight course, not wanting to collide with a horse's rump and get himself kicked.

"That you, George?" Pardee called from his harness room.

"Yes," Weaver said, "and I've brung you a drink."

When he went into the harness room, Pardee asked, "Did you find out about the stranger?"

Weaver nodded, and handed him a pint bottle of bourbon and said proudly, "After I told Quantrelle that Pat needed help he decided to go out there tomorrow. He's got the look of a good fightin' man, Joe — a ringtailed heller of a man."

Pardee took a long swig from the bottle and handed it to Weaver. "He's got the look, all right — but he wouldn't fight Hal Barton. How in hell do you figger that?"

Weaver shrugged. He took a drink and smacked his lips and said smilingly, "Nectar of the gods."

"Panther sweat," Pardee said. "That's what my drinkin' uncle always called it. He was a dilly, Uncle Hector."

A worried frown replaced the smile on Weaver's flushed face. "What am I goin' to do about Mae Bowen?" he asked. "She's gittin' worse, Joe — scarcely spoke to me at supper tonight. It purely hurts to have her treat me like that."

"Leave her be," Joe advised and motioned for his friend to sit beside him on the cot that served him for a bed. "There's a time for chasin' and a time for stayin' away. I've had three wives, at one time and another. I know how wimmin operate."

He reached for the bottle and took another swig. "Wimmin git queer notions in their noggins. You got to figger 'em different from the way you'd figger a man. They work just opposite, mostly. They'll damn a man for fightin' and they'll damn him if he don't. Same way with chasin'. When they git a man hooked they'll devil him by bein' standoffish. It's the way they're made, by God — contrary. My Uncle Hector gave me some good advice before I got married the first time, but I didn't pay him no heed. He said the only way to make a woman contented was to keep her barefoot and pregnant for the first five years. After that you've got yourself a real good wife."

George Weaver chuckled. "I can't hardly picture Mae barefooted nor pregnant either. But she'd make a wonderful wife, regardless."

Footsteps sounded in the barn doorway and now Hal Barton came into the harness-room and asked, "Is Quantrelle's horse still here?"

Pardee nodded, whereupon Barton said, "I'll be over at the Belvedere playing a little poker until midnight. If Quantrelle rides out let me know."

He glanced at Weaver, said derisively, "Drunk again," and went back out to the street.

George got up and staggered toward the door. "I'll show him I ain't drunk," he announced. "By God I've took too many insults from that smart aleck!"

But he went no farther than the doorway, and Joe Pardee said soothingly, "To hell with him, George. Let's me and you have another drink."

Quantrelle was up at daylight, thoroughly rested and eager for breakfast. Only a hardware drummer and the one-eyed blacksmith were in the diningroom when Mae Bowen took his order. She seemed more friendly this morning, asking, "Are you an old friend of George Weaver?"

"No," Quantrelle said, and seeing the disappointment in her eyes, asked, "Why?"

Mae shrugged. "I was hoping you were, and that perhaps you could talk George into doing his duty."

"Maybe he has no choice," Quantrelle suggested, liking her frankness. "Maybe his duty looks different to him than it does to you."

"How could it?" she demanded. "He's sheriff, isn't he? And the duty of a sheriff is to arrest wrongdoers, regardless of who they are?"

"Such as Pat Tanner?"

She nodded. She said in an emotional, low-toned voice, "I believe George is afraid of him," and went back to the kitchen.

When she served his breakfast Quantrelle said, "Being afraid of Apache Pat Tanner is nothing to be ashamed of, ma'am. I once saw a whole roomful of toughs back down in front of Tanner. He's a curly wolf for a fact."

"A sheriff," she said sharply, "should uphold the law or turn in his badge. One or the other. It's downright disgraceful the way people in town are talking about him. George Weaver used to be a popular man that everyone liked. But now they're ashamed to be seen talking to him on the street."

Quantrelle shrugged, and watching the upheaded way she walked to the kitchen, thought: *Mae wants her man to be a White Knight brave enough to tackle dragons barehanded.* She couldn't understand that any man worth his salt stood by his friends —

that George Weaver couldn't turn against Tanner just because others did. Women, he reflected, saw only one side of it — the side that affected them.

He paid his bill at the lobby desk, went out to the veranda and stood for a long moment giving the plaza a questing appraisal. Hal Barton, he supposed, would be on the watch for him. The Pool boss wouldn't want word of Gallatin's doublecrossing deal to reach Pat Tanner. Of course Barton didn't know he was a friend of Pat's, but even so he wouldn't feel easy about the bragging he'd done up there in the room. Quantrelle wondered if Barton was capable of shooting a man in the back, and guessed he was.

With that grim thought in mind, Quantrelle was warily alert as he crossed the sunlit plaza. Tailholt didn't seem the same to him today; it didn't even look the same. All sense of sanctuary had vanished so that now the town's very stillness seemed ominous — seemed tainted with a sense of foreboding. He eased up to the livery doorway half expecting to find Barton awaiting him. But it was Joe Pardee who stepped from a stall and asked, "You ridin' yonderly?"

Quantrelle nodded and gave the long, shadowed runway a brief inspection.

"Then you'd better keep your eyes peeled," Pardee warned. "Hal Barton rode out half an hour ago."

The warning surprised Quantrelle. "So you're Pat Tanner's friend," he suggested.

"Sort of a secret friend," Joe admitted. "A man in my business can't come right out and take sides."

Then he said, "Not meanin' to be overly bold I'd like to ask what made you take that tongue-lashin' from Barton yesterday."

Quantrelle grinned. Joe couldn't understand a man who rode a Chisum branded horse being so meek. "I'd had my fill of fighting," he explained. "I thought a feller could keep out of trouble if he refused to accept it. But I was wrong."

That seemed to please Joe Pardee. He grinned and loosed a quirt of tobacco juice and said, "I knowed it was somethin' like that, by God — I just knowed it!"

Quantrelle stood in thoughtful silence for a moment, considering what lay ahead of him. Hal Barton might be planning to drygulch him. The Pool boss might be desperate enough to do anything in order to keep him from telling Tanner what he knew . . .

As if thinking the same thing, Pardee said, "You could leave by way of the Benson road which goes due north, then turn into the cutoff trail about six miles from here. It would bring you back into the stageroad just east of Chalice's place."

"Might be a good idea," Quantrelle agreed, pleased at Pardee's kindness. A man got favors from unexpected places, he reflected, and climbing into saddle, said, "Much obliged, Joe."

The Tombstone stage rumbled into the plaza as Quantrelle rode from the barn. When it stopped in front of the Wells Fargo office he saw a passenger step down — a lanky, stoop-shouldered man with a heavy black mustache and bushy sideburns, garbed in range clothes. There was something familiar about him, Quantrelle thought; mildly curious he attempted to identify the man's face, but the newcomer turned abruptly away and went into a restaurant.

Quantrelle shrugged. Some casual acquaintance, he supposed. Riding up the dug road that climbed a steep slope north of town, he wondered if the years since Ellsworth had changed Apache Pat Tanner. The old Texan had seemed tough as bullhide, and as indestructible.

Afterward, while the bay shuffled along a dusty road that rimmed successive ridges,

Quantrelle eyed the roundabout range with a cowman's attention for grass and water and bean-clustered mesquite thickets. This, he decided, was excellent cattle country. The semi-arid slopes had been watered by summer showers so that now, in early autumn, there was graze and browse aplenty.

"Wouldn't mind running a little jag of cows here myself," he mused, and laughed at himself for such foolishness. A gunslick driver never got to own anything but memories . . .

Turning into the cutoff trail, Quantrelle held the bay to a walk, not wanting risen dust to reveal his passage. The west stageroad, he calculated, was no more than five or six miles south; perhaps less than that, depending upon the turnings of both trail and road. A man waiting down there might suspect a trick if he saw sign of westward travel on a little-used trail — might reset his ambush trap.

Recalling that he'd first seen Eve Chalice when she was talking with Barton, Quantrelle wondered how close a relationship existed between them. It might be merely a speaking acquaintance. But Barton possessed an aggressive manner that might appeal to women and he was handsome in a bold, broad-shouldered way. Quantrelle told himself that it made no difference to him; Eve would show no favors to a rider who sided Pat Tanner against the Pool. If she knew he had killed her brother she would hate him. The fact that Bob fired the first shot wouldn't matter in the least; she'd despise him, regardless.

But even so, knowing there wasn't a chance that he would ever hold Eve Chalice in his arms again, Quantrelle couldn't put her out of his mind. She was still there, like a pleasing and fantastic dream, when he came to a mailbox with a Cross Crescent. Halting here he eyed the adobe house, windmill and corrals which set back a short distance from the road. Eve, he supposed, was in that yonder house. The memory of her slow, sweet smile was a magnet strongly pulling him, so that he had to resist an impulse to stop by for a visit.

A witless, romantic fool, he thought disgustedly and rode on. He was almost to the Big T turnoff when Eve Chalice rode out of a stand of pines twenty yards ahead of him . . .

Quantrelle halted his horse once. He peered at her with a definite and increasing approval as she came up to him. It was an odd thing. She seemed more mature in riding clothes — more womanly, somehow, than in the conventional frills and furbelows of feminine attire. She wore a man's faded cotton shirt that couldn't conceal the twin swell of full, firm breasts. Snug fitting denim pants, tucked into the tops of cowboy boots, revealed the pleasing contour of supple thighs and slim hips.

He thought: *She's made the way a woman should be,* and saw the smile fade from her face.

"Don't women ever wear riding clothes in the country you come from?" she asked.

Quantrelle nodded, and nudged back the brim of his battered hat and said solemnly, "They do, ma'am — but not nearly so well."

And now they were both smiling as she said, "I've been waiting for you."

The surprise of that must have shown in Quantrelle's face, for she added quickly, "I heard about your trouble with Hal Barton, and that you might decide to take a job at Big T."

"So?" Quantrelle mused, admiring her frankness; admiring also the sunlit loveliness of her high-boned cheeks. A delicate dusting of tiny freckles across the bridge of her tip-tilted nose caught his attention and now he observed that her eyes were a blue-gray color, warm as campfire smoke.

"I hope you aren't going to work for Tanner," she said. "Even if you won't work for Barton I hope you aren't going to fight against the Pool."

Quantrelle asked, "Did your friend Barton tell why he hit me?"

"No, except to admit he was a trifle quick tempered."

Quantrelle smiled thinly. Eve, he supposed, wouldn't believe him if he told her that Barton had mistaken him for a man he was hiring as a spy — that the fight had been a sly trick to fool Pat Tanner. He said, "There was more to it than temper, ma'am. Much more."

Then he asked, "Why is the Pool so set against Tanner?"

"Because he has lorded it over Rincon Basin too darn long," she said emphatically. "Tanner elected George Weaver sheriff and makes no bones about owning him, body and soul. It's a disgrace the way Weaver refuses to lift a hand against Big T. Tanner won't let barbed wire come into the country. You'd think he owned all Rincon Basin, the way he makes the rules."

"It sounds," Quantrelle reflected, "as if Pat Tanner is a devil with horns."

"He may not have horns, but he's a devil," Eve insisted. "A stubborn old devil trying to be king of Rincon Basin — to run it as he sees fit, regardless of what the majority wants."

Then, as if to prove her point, she asked, "Do you suppose my father wants trouble? Why he's the most peaceable man in Arizona Territory. He dislikes fighting in all forms. He was crippled for life in a gun fight when he was young, and has hated shooting ever since. But now, well — he just hasn't any choice. The Pool needs men, and my brother is away from home, so Dad will have to fight, even though he hates it."

Mention of her brother stirred a sense of regret in Quantrelle, and a sense of guilt. Recalling the dead man's coarse, brutal features, he marveled that such a man should have so sweet-faced a sister. "How about Barton?" he asked. "Does Barton hate fighting also?"

That thinly veiled sarcasm brought a frowning gravity to Eve's face. "Hal," she defended, "is a doer — and a fighter too, when it's necessary. Perhaps he's too hot tempered at times, but most crusaders are high strung. He organized the Pool to protect six small ranches against Big T, and I admire him for it."

So she thinks he's a lily white crusader, Quantrelle thought, and noticed the engagement ring on her left hand. He said, "I see," and understood that there was more than admiration in her feeling for Hal Barton.

"The Pool must win this fight," Eve explained, as if eager to convince him. "It simply must. If we should lose it would mean bankruptcy for all of us — for men with wives and children. Whole families would be destitute."

Then, meeting his gaze directly, she asked, "Do you still intend to ride for Tanner?"

There was a moment when Quantrelle was tempted to tell her about Hal Barton's underhanded scheme — how the Pool boss had connived with Ike Gallatin to rig up a doublecross deal on Apache Pat. But he knew instinctively that none of this would impress Eve; that her only interest in him now was to keep a gunrider from increasing the odds against Barton's Pool. Added to that futility was the depressing sense of guilt — of playing the Judas role with a dead man's sister.

Finally he said, "I'm siding Pat Tanner. Nothing can change that, ma'am."

And because an expression of utter contempt came into Eve's eyes, he added soberly, "I wish it could be otherwise."

Then he rode on to the Big T turnoff and took it, not looking back.

Eve was turning in at the Cross Crescent gate when she saw Hal Barton come up the stageroad. She acknowledged his comradely salute and waited, conscious of the fine figure he made, sitting high and handsome on his big sorrel horse. There was a brash self-confidence in Hal that was catching; it had given less confident men the gumption to stand up against Big T. Even her father, who made a practice of avoiding trouble, had reacted to Hal's influence.

Now, as Barton rode up, he asked, "Is your Dad home, honey?"

Eve nodded, whereupon he grinned, saying, "Then I'll combine business with pleasure by kissing the future Mrs. Barton."

He leaned from saddle, kissing her in the confident fashion of a favored suitor. Eve thought: *He takes me for granted,* and gave him no more than passive acceptance — and resented his failure to notice this lack of response.

"I've decided the time has come to plan a definite campaign against Big T," Barton announced. "I want to talk it over with Jim."

Then he said, "I saw where someone rode

in from the cutoff trail. Did you see who it was?"

"Clay Quantrelle," Eve responded. "I talked to him." She wondered at the abrupt change in Hal's expression . . .

"You talked to him!" Barton exclaimed, seemingly shocked. "Why should you talk to a — a Lincoln County renegade like Clay Quantrelle?"

Eve couldn't understand his attitude. He had never seemed to be overly jealous; yet now he appeared angry, as if she had done an unfitting thing.

"I merely tried to talk him out of hiring on with Tanner," she explained. "I told him why the Pool was bucking Big T — that it was a matter of survival for men with families."

"And what did he tell you?" Barton asked impatiently.

"That he would ride for Tanner, regardless."

"That all he said?"

Eve nodded.

Barton smiled, and Eve saw an expression in his eyes now that was like relief as he said amusedly, "You should've known it was useless, honey. Saddle tramps always sign on with warrior outfits. Quantrelle wants the gun wages Tanner will pay. That's all he's interested in."

Eve considered that as they rode toward the house. "Perhaps," she said, "but he didn't act happy about it. In fact he seemed sorry."

Clay Quantrelle followed a deep-rutted road through timbered hills and across wide, grassy meadows. This was Big T range and it seemed odd that he hadn't been challenged. Surely Pat Tanner wouldn't be so careless as to leave his front gate unguarded. Thinking of the wagonload of provisions he'd seen leaving town yesterday, Quantrelle wondered if the crew had started out on roundup this morning; if that was why no rider had intercepted him.

Then, as his horse labored up a steep, wall-like ridge, Quantrelle had his answer. A redhaired rider, awaiting him on the bald crest, asked brashly, "Where you goin' pilgrim?"

"Big T," Quantrelle answered, easing a trifle to the right so that this guard could read the bay's brand without trouble. Recalling Sheriff Weaver's tally of Tanner's crew, Quantrelle decided at once that this was Red Parmalee. A lookout here would have an unobstructed view for miles; he wondered if Red had seen the meeting with Eve

Chalice, and guessed he had . . .

"What's your business at Big T?" Parmalee demanded, a suspicious frown on his freckled, bold-featured face.

A sardonic smile eased Quantrelle's lips. This was what range war did to a country. It banished all semblance of hospitality. There was no welcome for trail-weary travelers; no courtesy nor tolerance to strangers. Every man was a potential enemy until proved otherwise.

"I'm a friend of Apache Pat's," Quantrelle said.

"You be?"

Quantrelle nodded, and started to ride on.

"Not so goddam fast!" Parmalee objected. "I seen you talkin' to Jim Chalice's girl."

"Any law against that?" Quantrelle inquired.

"How do I know you're a friend of Pat's?" Parmalee demanded.

"Because I told you so," Quantrelle said. Looking Red in the eye he started around him on the left and kept his right hand close to holster.

That confused Parmalee. He turned his horse as if to block the bay's passage, then changed his mind and just sat there, not knowing what he should do.

"If there's any doubt in your mind about

me being Pat's friend, come along and see for yourself," Quantrelle suggested.

Then he rode on across the ridge, not looking back. Red Parmalee, he guessed, wasn't too sure of himself as a gunslick. Like a lot of tough young riders, Red got a trifle confused in the clutch. Or so it had seemed . . .

Presently, as the trail tipped down the north slope, Quantrelle had his look at Big T. The square adobe house, surrounded by sheds and corrals, lay on a flat mesa directly below this ridge. It had the impressive appearance of a headquarters spread. "A real cow outfit," Quantrelle mused admiringly.

He was halfway down the steep slope when two shots sounded behind and above him. Looking back he saw Parmalee on the rim, and understood that the redhead had taken this means of signalling his approach to the ranch. Then, as Quantrelle reached the mesa's lower level, a rider loped from the ranch yard, meeting him half way — a reedy, dark-skinned man who peered at him with black, appraising eyes and asked, "Lookin' for somebody?"

Quantrelle nodded, and guessed that this was Ike Gallatin. If it was, Gallatin might be expecting Barton's spy and be waiting for him to give some sign. As if in answer to that thought, the reedy rider grinned and said, "I'm foreman here, name of Gallatin."

The sure knowledge that he was looking at a double-crosser stirred a swift sense of dislike in Quantrelle. A man would have to be lower than snake sign in a wheel rut to play the dirty game this ramrod was playing . . .

"I'm looking for Pat Tanner," Quantrelle said, and observing the way Gallatin eyed his scarred cheek, laughed a little to himself. The foreman was waiting for him to divulge his mission — to mention Barton, or the Wyatt who'd sent him to Rincon Basin. *Probably thinks I'm being stupid,* Quantrelle thought amusedly, sensing Gallatin's impatience.

But the dark ramrod was playing it cautious. He asked, "Did you come through Tailholt?" and was waiting for a reply when a massive, gray-haired man rode out from the yard.

Ignoring Gallatin's question, Quantrelle called, "Howdy, Pat."

Tanner cuffed back his flat-crowned sombrero. His eyes, an almost colorless gray in contrast to shaggy black brows and a face weather-honed to deep mahogany, contemplated Quantrelle for a full moment before he exclaimed, "Quantrelle, by God — Clay

78

Quantrelle!"

Quantrelle glanced at Gallatin, seeing this man's mystification and enjoying it. Ike didn't know what to make of it . . .

Tanner rode up with a broad grin bracketing his arrogant, square-lipped mouth. He leaned from saddle and shook hands and boomed, "By God I'm glad to see you, son — gladder than six Sonora steers at a feed trough!"

He hadn't changed at all, Quantrelle thought. Towering above medium-sized men like a windmill in the brush, Apache Pat's big body was straight as a lodgepole pine, and the grip of his rope-calloused fingers was as crushing as it had been that night he'd said goodbye in Ellsworth. Five years hadn't changed him at all.

"Heard you're having a little trouble," Quantrelle said, and noticed that Gallatin was riding back to the yard.

"More goddam trouble than you could shake a stick at," Tanner admitted. There was no complaint in his booming voice, though; if anything there was a note of bragging, as if trouble was a thing he was proud to cope with — a sporting proposition that he welcomed with the relish of a skilled and prideful competitor. Where other men might grumble or complain, or whine about their unhappy lot, Pat Tanner practically boasted about his trouble.

As they walked their horses toward the yard, Apache Pat said smilingly, "I battled the goddam Apaches to a standstill and I'll do the same with Barton's rag-tag Pool."

Quantrelle contemplated the fort-like adobe house, observing that its windows were small and high from the ground. The walls, he judged, were at least two feet thick, with heavy log beams protruding all along the front and forming a roof for the gallery. "It looks," he reflected, "like you were expecting trouble when you built your house."

"I was — and got it," Tanner boomed, chuckling with the memory of that trouble. "Rincon Basin was crawlin' with Apaches at that time. The brush was full of 'em. Old Cochise raided me a dozen different times, but his mangy braves never got inside. And neither will Hal Barton's bunch."

Quantrelle glanced at Gallatin who had dismounted at the horse corral. "One of Barton's bunch isn't far from being in your house right now," he said, and when Tanner peered at him, added, "It's a long story, Pat. Let's hunt us some shade before I tell it."

Ike Gallatin tied his horse to the corral

fence. He glanced at the three men who were struggling with a green bronc preparatory to putting shoes on the critter, then watched Apache Pat and Quantrelle take chairs on the front gallery. A sharp sense of suspicion prodded Gallatin; a queerly urgent sense of foreboding. If Quantrelle was an old friend of Tanner's he couldn't be the man Barton had sent. Still, Quantrelle looked like a gunslinger, and there was a scar on his face . . .

A startling thought came to Gallatin now: Suppose Quantrelle *had* been sent here by Barton, who didn't know he was Tanner's friend? Suppose Quantrelle knew Big T's foreman was in cahoots with the Pool!

Apprehension ran through Ike Gallatin, the thrust of it so strong now that he led his horse around back of the house. Apache Pat Tanner would show no mercy to a double-crosser, and neither would the crew. A man wouldn't have a chance. Tanner would gut-shoot a traitor and laugh while he groaned himself to death.

Gallatin considered riding off now, while there was time. But indecision gripped him. Quantrelle might not be the man Barton had sent — might not know anything about the rigged-up deal here. In which case there'd be no reason for running.

Abruptly then Gallatin made his decision. Removing his spurs he hung them on his saddlehorn, tied his horse to the back stoop railing and went into the kitchen where Gramp Pettigrue was preparing supper. "Did that load of supplies fix you with all the groceries you'll need for roundup?" Gallatin inquired casually.

The old cook nodded, asked, "Who's the new man jawin' with Pat on the gallery?"

Gallatin shrugged. "Some drifter named Quantrelle," he said, and walked on into the livingroom.

Voices came to Gallatin as he stepped cautiously across the big room; Quantrelle's voice, and then Apache Pat's loud profanity. When Gallatin eased up to one side of the doorway he heard Tanner exclaim, "I been suspicious that Ike was up to somethin' but I couldn't catch the stinkin' son. By God I'll rope his gut-shot carcass across a saddle and have it delivered to Barton's ranch with a note tied to one of his ears, sayin' here's your stray dog."

Ike Gallatin shivered. He tiptoed back across the livingroom with his right hand close to holster. And because Hal Barton had as good as signed his death warrant, he cursed the bungling boss of the Rincon Pool . . .

Out on front gallery Quantrelle said, "I dislike being an informer, Pat. Especially if it costs a man his life. Why not just fire Gallatin?"

"And have him fightin' us, tooth and nail!" Tanner scoffed. "There's only one way to treat a goddam rattlesnake — stomp him while you got the chance!"

The old cowman strode to the gallery step, nudging his Peacemaker so that it rested loosed in holster. "Ike!" he called, peering toward the corral. "Ike Gallatin!"

"Are you going to give him a chance to draw?" Quantrelle asked, not liking this.

"Hell no," Tanner said with hushed fury. "I'm goin' to chop him down same as I'd chop a goddam snake."

Quantrelle frowned, knowing that a doublecrosser rated no mercy, yet inwardly flinching at the thought that his report would cause so cold-blooded an execution.

"Ike!" Tanner yelled, his bull-toned voice carrying to the corral where a man called back, "He ain't here, Pat."

"Then go find him," Tanner ordered. "Git a move on!"

The cowboy climbed the corral fence and had one leg thrown over the top rail preparatory to jumping down when he abruptly flung out an arm in a pointing gesture and yelled, "There goes Ike now."

Quantrelle turned, saw a horseman ride up the ridge trail, traveling at a hard run.

Pat Tanner cursed, ran into the house and came out with a rifle. But Gallatin had already disappeared over the rim. "The dirty son!" he raged. "The dirty, doublecrossin' son!"

CHAPTER THREE

There wasn't much talk at the supper table. The Big T crew seemed too surprised and shocked to discuss Gallatin's treachery. But afterward, while all hands sat smoking on the front gallery, Red Parmalee said, "I thought Ike acted sort of spooky when he rode past, sayin' he was makin' a quick trip to town."

Kid Calhoun, who'd been shaving less than a month and tried to conceal his lack of years with a swaggering toughness, declared, "I'll put a slug in Gallatin first time we meet."

"Per-aps not," Sonora suggested, a humorless smile on his round, pock-pitted face. "Ike ees *pronto* weeth the right hand — *muy pronto.*"

Quantrelle observed that Jim Jeddy hadn't uttered a word all evening. The bald-headed little rider seemed content to puff on his pipe and listen. Mild-mannered and shy to the point of seeming afraid of his own shadow, Jeddy appeared out of place among these tough talking men. But Apache Pat had referred to the meek little rider as a "ringtailed heller with a shootin' iron."

When the crew had drifted off to the bunkhouse, Quantrelle asked, "Isn't there a chance of settling your trouble with the Pool by some peaceful means, Pat?"

Tanner laughed. "By God that's good! Did you ever hear of a proddy stud bein' casterated by peaceful means?"

And when Quantrelle shook his head, Apache Pat announced, "Well, that's what Hal Barton is — a high-tailed proddy stud and he's plannin' to be boss of Rincon Basin. I don't mean just head man of the Pool — I mean boss of the whole shebang whereby he'll control every inch of range and probably end up ownin' it. One way and another he's got 'em all convinced they should help him take over. To show you how slick he is, Barton talked Jim Chalice into over-stockin' his range with Mex steers, then lent Jim money to keep him from losin' his place when the beef market went to hell. Up till then Jim's daughter hadn't given Barton much of a tumble, bein' a real nice girl and smarter than most. But after Barton lent Jim that money she let the smooth-jawed son talk her into takin' his engagement ring. He's slicker'n cow slobbers, that Barton."

So that was how the Pool boss had won himself a favored place in Eve's affections. No wonder she thought Barton was God's gift to womanhood; he had saved her home when there'd been no help from a fiddle-footed brother . . .

"I ran this country for fifteen years without no real trouble," Apache Pat explained. "Of course there was some rustlin' and we had to string up a greasy-sack thief or two, just as warnin' to the others. But things was goin' along all right until Barton came in with his loco notions of criss-crossin' the range with barb wire. Once you do that you'll have sodbusters all over the place tryin' to grow crops along with cattle. Then what happens? The dim-witted sodbusters go broke in three–four years and move out. But they've ruint the graze for the rest of us, and so in the end we go busted too. Nobody wins. Everybody loses. I tried to tell Jim Chalice that, and the rest of them. They're all cowmen and should savvy what I said. But by God they didn't, and now it's me — or them."

Mention of Chalice reminded Quantrelle of what Eve had said about Tanner's brash tactics. He asked, "Hasn't the Pool tried to bring in another load of wire since you burned that freight wagon?"

"No, because they ain't got the cash. And I didn't burn that wagon. My crew was home that night."

Quantrelle couldn't comprehend it. If Big T hadn't burned the wagon, who had? And why? Then an idea came to him and he asked, "How about Ike Gallatin? Was he here that night also?"

Tanner nodded. Then he said, "Well, I suppose Ike was here. But he could've been away without me knowin'."

Quantrelle built a cigarette and lit it, his face showing a satisfied smile in the match flare. "The wagon burning turned a lot of folks against you," he mused thoughtfully. "Until that happened the people in town were inclined to favor Big T, instead of the Pool. Well, it's my guess that Barton and Gallatin framed it for the purpose of turning opinion against you."

"But the load of wire cost a lot of money," Tanner objected. "So damn much money that they ain't been able to buy another batch, or pay their bills in town. By God it just about broke most of them. Why in hell would Barton waste Pool money like that?"

Quantrelle considered the question in

silence for a long moment. It didn't seem reasonable that Barton would deliberately bankrupt the Pool. But someone had burned the wagon, and Apache Pat said his crew hadn't done it.

Finally Quantrelle suggested, "Perhaps Barton thought it was worth that much to turn the town against you, Pat. In any case I'm glad you didn't do the job."

"Why?"

"Because I'd dislike working for a bush-whack outfit."

Tanner chuckled. He reached over and slapped Quantrelle's shoulder and said, "You may be doin' worse than that before this rumpus is settled. The real trouble will probably start day after tomorrow when we begin gatherin' beef. Barton knows my credit has run out in town and that my only way of gittin' cash is to deliver a bunch of steers in Benson. He'll most likely try to stop us, one way or another."

For a time they smoked in silence. A gentle breeze brought its cool hint of on-coming winter off the high Kettle Drums, and propelled the windmill to slow clank-ing. A cow bawled somewhere on the dark flats, and over in the bunkhouse Red Par-malee sang a verse of *Black-Eyed Susie* in a raw, hooting voice.

"That jigger should be up on Look Out Ridge," Apache Pat grumbled. "His stint runs to midnight, with time out for supper."

Quantrelle got up, feeling the need for movement. "I'll finish out his stint, Pat. Got so much sleep last night I feel like taking some night air just for the hell of it."

"Suit yourself, but it ain't necessary. Red's a reg'lar damn nighthawk anyway."

Quantrelle went over to the corral and saddled his bay. When he rode back past the house he stopped in front of Tanner and asked, "Had any unwelcome visitors at night so far?"

"Not lately, but I got a hunch Barton's bunch is primed for trouble."

"How about Weaver," Quantrelle asked. "Will he stick, if it gets rough?"

"Sure, but that don't matter much," Tanner said. He chuckled, adding, "Weaver makes me a good sheriff. He's so goddam yellow he goes off and hides every time he hears shooting."

Quantrelle was thinking about that as he rode up the ridge trail. Eve Chalice had called the turn exactly when she said Tanner made no bones about owning Sheriff Weaver. The old cowman took George's loyalty as a matter of course.

The same as mine, Quantrelle thought and grinned, thinking how tough an old tyrant he'd thrown in with. Apache Pat belonged to the Texas breed that would charge hell on a foundered horse with a bucket of water.

For half an hour, while he sat with one leg draped comfortably across the saddle's fork, Quantrelle heard no sound of travel. He couldn't distinguish Cross Crescent's lamp-lit windows because of intervening timber, but there was a remote beacon of light due east, and another dimly showing far to the south. The homes of Pool members, he supposed — of men who'd banded together for the express purpose of busting Big T.

Recalling Eve's denunciation of Tanner, Quantrelle thought: *She sees only one side of it.* And at this moment he heard the remote rumor of a horse on the trail below him.

Instantly alert, Quantrelle eased his horse into the shadow of a large boulder, drew his gun and waited. There was a quarter crescent of moon that played hide and seek with high scudding clouds; it was out now, casting a soft light across the ridge crest. Who, he wondered, would be rimming around at this time of night? It occurred to him that the oncoming rider might be Ike Gallatin wanting to vent his spite on Apache Pat.

Quantrelle grinned, thinking the ex-ramrod had a surprise in store for him.

The yonder horse climbed to the crest, giving Quantrelle his first vague glimpse of a rider that seemed too short to be Ike Gallatin. Quantrelle waited until no more than a dozen yards separated them, then called, "Who's that?"

"It's me — Fern," a feminine voice announced. "Is that you, Red?"

Quantrelle sighed and lowered his gun. *Red's sweet stuff come a-calling,* he thought. "No, ma'am," he announced. "I'm taking Red's place."

The girl came on until she was directly in front of him. "I thought this was Red's night to be here," she said, a huge disappointment in her voice.

Her eyes seemed very large and dark against the pallor of a heart-shaped face. She looked like a blubbering kid ready to cry. She wore a cheap cotton dress, the skirt of which was hiked up by the saddle, exposing one black-stockinged thigh.

"Something important you wanted to see Red about?" Quantrelle asked.

She nodded, leaning forward to peer into his shadowed face. "I thought you were Jim Jeddy," she said. "Who are you?"

"A new man, name of Quantrelle."

For a moment she considered him in thoughtful silence. Then, as if prompted by an urgency that overcame pride or reluctance, she said, "Please tell Red to stop by at the house tomorrow night, sure. It's important."

With a girlish note of pleading, she added, "I'll be much obliged if you'd give Red my message in private. It — it might cause talk if others heard it."

"Sure," Quantrelle agreed. "That's how it'll be — strictly private."

"Thanks," she murmured and rode back the way she had come, her horse's hoofs making a lonely sound against the night's vast silence. And because Clay Quantrelle had seen other girls come looking for their lovers, he thought: *The same old story.*

Ten miles southeast of Look Out Ridge, Hal Barton sat in his log house talking to Ike Gallatin. "It was a natural mistake," the Pool boss explained. "Wyatt wrote that the fellow would show up about now, a big drifter with a scar on one cheek. Quantrelle filled that description, and refused to take a job with the Pool — same as it was planned. That's why I was so sure he was the right man."

"Well, your mistake damn near cost me

my hide," Gallatin muttered frowningly. "And it cost us our ace in the hole at Big T. Couldn't you of kept him from runnin' to Tanner with his story?"

Barton shrugged. "I waited for him on the stageroad, but the sly devil went around by the cutoff and got by me. He's smart, Ike — smart and dangerous."

He thought for a moment, one eye squinted and his forehead rutted by a tapered, v-shaped wrinkle. "I stopped by to see Chalice. He's still spooky about raiding Tanner's roundup crew. But I'll figure a way to make him feel different about it."

"What about me?" Gallatin asked. "What do I do now?"

Barton considered the question so long that Ike demanded, "Well, how about it?"

"Lay low until tomorrow night," Barton suggested. "I've got an idea this thing is going to work out all for the best. We don't need an ace in the hole at Big T. All we need is a scapegoat, and we've got him."

"Who?" Gallatin asked.

"Quantrelle," Barton said and smiled confidently. "There's more than one way to skin a cat, Ike. We've got to change our plans a trifle, but we'll skin the same cat."

It was mid-afternoon before Quantrelle had

a chance to talk to Red Parmalee in private. Most of the morning had been spent in the horse corral, getting the *remuda* ready for tomorrow's start of the roundup. Now, as Parmalee went to the wagonshed for a fresh supply of horseshoe nails, Quantrelle intercepted him and said, "A girl named Fern came up to the ridge last night and asked me to deliver a message to you."

Red grinned, revealing a chaser's vanity. "She's a great one for rimmin' around in the moonlight," he bragged. "Best little night rider west of the Pecos."

"She said for you to stop by the house this evening, and to tell you it's important."

Parmalee shook his head, saying, "She ought to know better. Her old man run me off with a gun, last time I was there. Fern must think I'm dim witted. Fun is fun, but it ain't worth gittin' shot at, by God."

He chuckled, adding, "That's a woman for you. They'll tantalize a man and play hard to catch. Then when you catch 'em they do the chasin'."

"She didn't look like a woman to me," Quantrelle said, not smiling. "She looked like a worried girl."

Red winked at him. "She's more woman than you'd think friend. Them young ones catch on fast and they can sure make a man git a wiggle on hisself."

He went on into the wagonshed then, smiling at the memory of past pleasure . . .

Quantrelle shrugged and returned to the front gallery where Apache Pat was repairing a pair of ancient bullhide chaps. Red wasn't so old himself — not more than twenty-three or so — but he seemed to be an old hand at the romance game. No telling how many worried girls he'd left behind in his free-lance philandering.

By supper time the hundred and one odd chores that invariably precede a roundup were completed. The *remuda* was fresh shod and most of the green broncs topped off; the chuckwagon was loaded with provisions, water kegs caulked, tarps mended, harness repaired — all the necessary chores that made up the usual preparation. The crew was in high spirits, and even Tanner seemed a trifle excited by the impending gather. For this was more than just a roundup — it was a contest for survival of an old established cow outfit faced with bankruptcy.

"We'll rim the Kettle Drums and work back," Apache Pat announced. "Don't bother with she-stuff and calves. All we're after is beef — the quicker the better."

Afterward, sitting on the gallery with him, Quantrelle asked, "How many head you figure on gathering for the trail herd?"

"Depends on how long it takes, and how much trouble Barton's bunch give us. It's a trifle early for shippin' and the price ain't what it should be, which means I won't git near what I should for the beef I sell."

He got up, stepping over to a gallery post and knocked ashes from the bowl of his pipe. "It'll take five, six hundred head at least to get the cash I need to keep goin'."

And in this instant, as he turned back toward Quantrelle, a bullet slammed him in the chest.

Quantrelle heard the meaty impact which was echoed by a rifle's sharp report — and by two more bullets that whined wickedly past him. Ducking away from the window's shaft of lamplight, Quantrelle fired four shots at the brief bloom of muzzle flame across the dark yard, then reloaded his gun and heard Red Parmalee yell from the bunkhouse: "Who's shootin?"

Instead of answering Quantrelle eased along the gallery. High banked clouds obscured the moon as he stepped down and moved swiftly across the dark yard. The rifle, he believed, had been fired by Ike Gallatin. And he suspected the ex-ramroad was waiting out there for another target to be outlined against lamplight.

Quantrelle thought: *Gramp Pettigrue should put out that goddam lamp!* He heard men moving over near the bunkhouse, and now Kid Calhoun's excited voice demanding, "Where's Pat?"

Quantrelle scanned the yonder gloom, expecting to see another flare of muzzle flame and wanting to target that beacon. But it didn't come and presently he detected the remote tromp of a horse going up the ridge trail. Gallatin, he reflected grimly, had done his dirty work and was departing.

Quantrelle cursed and turned back toward the house, anxious to know how bad Apache Pat was hurt, and now glimpsed a vague shape moving away from the windmill. His first thought was that one of the crew was prowling the yard, as he had done. But it occurred to him that the yonder man would've heard the hoofbeats on the trail the same as he, and reached the same conclusion. Yet the fellow wasn't going toward the house; *he was going away from it.*

Tilting up his gun, Quantrelle called sharply, "Stop right there!"

He heard the skulker loose a gusty breath, dimly saw his unmoving shape, and thought: *He can see me also.* Expecting a shot, Quantrelle dropped to one knee, his gun cocked for firing. But the man called nervously, "Don't shoot!"

That surprised Quantrelle. He had expected the intruder to try any trick rather than be captured.

"Light a match," Quantrelle ordered, and when the man obeyed, said, "Drop your gun so I can see it fall."

Kid Calhoun came off the front gallery, calling, "Where you at, Quantrelle?"

"Over here," Quantrelle directed, "and I've got company."

"You mean — Gallatin?" Calhoun asked excitedly.

"No. Move off to the left, while I herd this jasper into the light."

The match had burned out, and now the man asked, "You want me to go to the house?"

"Yes," Quantrelle said, and when the fellow began walking, Quantrelle moved over to pick up the gun he'd dropped. Sniffing its barrel, he thought: *It wasn't him.*

The gun hadn't been fired, which seemed odd. Why should a man accompany Gallatin here on a sneak raid and not take a shot at targets plainly outlined against lamplight? It didn't make sense.

Kid Calhoun, watching in front of the house, demanded, "What you doin' here,

Mister Swenson?"

"My business," Swenson said sourly, "and none of yours."

He turned and faced Quantrelle, his frowning, age-seamed face fully revealed in the doorway's shaft of lamplight. "I didn't do that shootin'," he said. "It was somebody else."

Ignoring the declaration, Quantrelle said, "Watch him, Kid," and hurried into the house.

They had Apache Pat on a bed. His face was ashen, his eyes closed. Gramp Pettigrue bent over him, fashioning a bandage; Jim Jeddy, Sonora and Parmalee stood watching in the rigidly grave fashion of men stunned by calamity.

"How bad is it?" Quantrelle demanded.

"Awful bad," Red muttered. "He's a goner, for sure."

"No he ain't neither," Gramp Pettigrue objected crossly. "I've saw him hurt this bad before and he got over it."

"I'll go get a doctor," Quantrelle said and hurried outside.

Kid Calhoun, standing with his gun drawn, asked, "What we goin' to do with Mister Swenson?"

Quantrelle shrugged, not knowing the answer to that question, and not much caring. But presently, while he saddled the bay gelding, he called across the yard, "Go with Swenson while he gets his horse, Kid. I'm taking him to town."

When Quantrelle rode over to the gallery, Swenson was in saddle. The old man said, "Look at my gun and you'll see it ain't been fired."

"I know that already," Quantrelle muttered. He climbed into saddle and said, "Lead off and ride fast. I'm in a hurry."

"You got no right —"

Quantrelle drew his gun, rode in beside Swenson and asked impatiently, "You going to ride to town or do you want to be toted?"

Swenson rode. When they halted their horses for a breather on the crest of the ridge, he said, "I don't know who done that shootin' and I don't care. Whoever it was, he came after I got into the yard."

"And what were you doing there?" Quantrelle asked, convinced that Swenson had come with Gallatin.

"Waitin' for a shot at Red Parmalee," Swenson said. "I'd of got it, too, if I had to wait all night."

Astonished by that bald admission, Quantrelle asked, "Why you gunning for Red?"

"On account of what he done to my girl," Swenson muttered. "I just found out today.

She's — by God she's goin' to have a baby!"

Quantrelle loosed a sighing curse. "You sure it's Red?" he asked.

"Sure I'm sure. Didn't I run him off a dozen times durin' the past six months? Didn't I catch 'em hidin' in the brush like a pair of rabbits in breedin' season? I knowed Parmalee was no damn good, but my girl wouldn't listen to me."

The plain misery in his voice convinced Quantrelle. He said, "I'm sorry mister — real sorry." As they rode on across the ridge, he asked, "Would your daughter marry Red, if he asked her?"

Swenson grunted. "No chance of that," he muttered. "Them Big T gunslingers ain't quittin' high wages to marry a homesteader's daughter."

"Red will," Quantrelle promised. "He'll marry your daughter within the next two or three days."

Swenson didn't seem to hear that. He said miserably, "Fern was a good girl until that studdy scamp started pesterin' her. She was a proud and proper girl."

Then, as if finally absorbing what Quantrelle had said, he asked doubtingly, "What makes you say Red would marry her?"

"Because I'll tell him to," Quantrelle muttered. Then, riding on past Swenson, he cautioned, "Don't go gunning for your future son-in-law," and spurred the bay to a run.

Sheriff George Weaver sat alone on the Empire Hotel veranda smoking his second cigar since supper. It was past eleven o'clock now and there was nothing else to do, except go up to his cheerless room. Or go over to the Belvedere and get drunk again. But he was still shaky as an aspen from the binge night before last. He'd got so drunk that Joe Pardee had to help him up to his room.

There had been a time when Mae Bowen used to sit here with him of an evening; when they'd made fine plans for the future. She had hugged him and kissed him, sitting on his lap in this very chair, time after time, with the woman smell of her making him rampageous as a ridge-running stud. But that was before a wagonload of barb wire had been ambushed — before the people of this town had turned against Big T, and against their sheriff for failing to arrest Apache Pat Tanner.

Weaver sighed, recalling how insistently Mae had endeavored to convince him that he should either arrest Tanner or turn in his badge. She hadn't seemed to understand that there was no real evidence against Apache Pat, and that he couldn't have arrested the old hellion if there had been. You could kill a man like Tanner, if you outdrew him; but you sure as hell couldn't arrest him. He was that kind of a man.

"A ring-tailed heller from here to who hid the broom," Weaver muttered and felt an old envy. How, he wondered, did some men get to be like that — like they just didn't give a damn, one way or the other, about dying? It didn't seem possible a human being could feel that way. Any normal person should be afraid of death. But Tanner wasn't. Apache Pat, he guessed, must have been born with the fear part of his brain missing. Either that or he'd been weaned on wild mustang milk.

But George hadn't been able to explain it to Mae. She just sniffed and said, "Tanner may talk and act like a brass-riveted king, but he's just a man. So are you, and a sheriff besides."

He had tried to explain the practical side of politics to Mae, telling her that he'd been elected only because of Tanner's backing, and so couldn't turn against him. But Mae couldn't understand why that should make any difference. And at the last she had called him a "tin-star coward."

Maybe I am, Weaver thought, and had a hankering for the bottle of Colonel's Monogram in his room. A man couldn't change himself from the way he was made. Some men were born brave and some weren't. And a man couldn't ramrod life; he had to take it the way it came. No matter how goddam lonely the long nights were, or how dismal the days. But he could make it bearable by keeping himself half drunk most of the time . . .

A rider galloped into town from the west, crossed the plaza and dismounted at the Belvedere hitchrack. When he went through the batwing gates Weaver got a glimpse of his face and asked himself, "Now what would Ike Gallatin be doin' in town at this time of night?"

Over at the livery Joe Pardee came out, stood on his bench and blew out the lantern that hung in the doorway. Weaver thought about going over to have a little talk with Joe in the harness room. But he didn't feel like walking that far, with the shakes and all.

Weaver got up and was turning to go into the hotel lobby when Gallatin came out of the saloon with Hal Barton and a stranger. George peered at the trio in mild astonishment, wondering what Ike was doing with the Rincon Pool boss. It didn't make sense for Big T's foreman to be associating with Tanner's arch enemy. No sense at all.

"Mebbe I'm still drunk," Weaver muttered, scratching his head.

But now, as the three of them came directly toward the hotel, Weaver understood that he wasn't imagining a thing. It was real, and there was something in the wind — something unusual. He walked over to the steps and was standing there when Hal Barton announced, "Ike says Tanner turned on him, and he shot Tanner in self-defense."

The impact of those words held George Weaver speechless. Apache Pat Tanner shot! And by his own foreman . . .

"What happened?" Weaver demanded. "Why did Pat turn on you, Ike?"

"Because I didn't want him to hire that Lincoln County killer Quantrelle. Me and Pat had words, and I quit. I was asaddle, ready to ride out, when Tanner throwed a tantrum. He talked like a wild man, sayin' if I didn't ride for Big T I wouldn't ride for nobody else. He grabbed for his gun. I jumped my horse around and Tanner's slug went past me. Then I fired at him and hightailed for the tules."

"I'll be damned," Weaver muttered, unable to wholly absorb so monstrous a circumstance. "Beats anythin' I ever heard of."

Then he asked, "What makes you think Quantrelle is a Lincoln County killer?"

"Go ask Joe Pardee what brand is on Quantrelle's horse," Barton suggested.

"He'll tell you it's John Chisum's," Gallatin said, "and I'm tellin' you that Quantrelle is just a goddam, no-good drifter on the dodge, not fit for decent folks to associate with."

"How bad is Apache Pat hurt?" Weaver asked.

"Couldn't say," Gallatin muttered. Then he chuckled, adding, "I didn't wait around to find out. And to tell you the truth I don't give a damn. Not after the way he pulled that gun on me. Mebbe he's dead, for all I know. Serve him right if he was."

Hal Barton peered narrowly at the sheriff, saying, "You aren't going to arrest Ike, are you, George?"

It wasn't a question. It was a declaration — a bald statement of fact. Weaver's glance shifted from Barton to Gallatin and then to the tall stranger with the black mustache. For a hushed moment, while they eyed him unblinkingly, Weaver said nothing. This, he understood, was Hal Barton's way of telling him the Pool wouldn't stand for Ike Gallatin's arrest.

"If it was self defense there's no call for it," Weaver said finally.

But Barton wasn't satisfied. He said with arrogant assurance, "No matter what it was, or what they try to call it, you aren't arresting Ike. That's sure, George, and don't make any mistake about it. You've loafed through all the trouble up till now, refusing to lift a hand against Big T's lawless acts. Now you keep right on loafing, no matter what happens."

"Either that," Gallatin suggested, "or turn in your badge."

The lanky stranger asked, "Is that what he's got pinned to his vest?"

And then he laughed.

But George Weaver paid no heed. He said, "I've got to go get Doc Elliott and send him out there quick."

He ran toward Residential Avenue, afraid that Apache Pat might be dying, or already dead; and knowing he was through in Rincon Basin if the old cowman died.

Clay Quantrelle was well beyond Cross Crescent when he met a buggy coming along the dark road at a rapid pace. He pulled off to one side, giving his tired horse a breather while the rig passed, then loped on toward town. Even though Parmalee was convinced that Apache Pat didn't have a chance, Gramp Pettigrue thought otherwise; and he might be right. Men like Apache Pat took a lot of killing.

Tanner's death, Quantrelle reflected, would end the range war. With him out of the way there'd be no one to obstruct Hal Barton's fence-building programme. Big T would pass on to other hands — some relative perhaps, or a Tucson bank, depending on Apache Pat's financial obligations. But, Quantrelle thought grimly, the trouble wouldn't be over for him. There'd still be one gun chore to do; a debt of vengeance to pay. If Apache Pat died there would be a score to settle with Ike Gallatin.

Recalling all that Tanner had told him, Quantrelle swore dejectedly. Even if the old cowman lived, the prospects of winning were poor now. For Big T's credit had run out in Tailholt. Every pound of provisions Tanner had bought at the Mercantile had to be paid for in cash; every cartridge, can of gun grease or block of salt. And Pat had spent his last dollar on that load of provisions three days ago.

"We'll drive a herd of steers to Benson some time next week," Pat had explained. "I'll have to take whatever price I can git, just so it's cash on the barrel-head. My crew has missed a couple of paydays. I don't want 'em missin' meals besides."

Now the trail drive would be postponed — perhaps never be made.

Remembering that Swenson had referred to Big T riders as earning high wages, Quantrelle smiled cynically. The crew wouldn't even be eating regularly a week from now. It occurred to him that he had let sympathy get the best of him when he promised Swenson that Red would marry his pregnant daughter. A man had no right butting in on a deal like that. For all he knew Fern might be a swivel-hipped teaser deserving what she'd got. She should have recognized Red for what he was — a foot-loose man wanting some fun in the moonlight. And she had probably wanted it also. But there had been heartbreak in the old man's voice, and a shame that had turned him berserk.

Quantrelle muttered flatly, "So Red marries her," and shrugged off the complications such a marriage would bring. Keeping the bay to a steady lope he went down the dug road into Tailholt.

Except for the saloon, and a dim shaft of lamplight at the hotel doorway, the plaza was dark. Pitch black. He passed the livery and was going by the hotel when Sheriff

Weaver called from the veranda, "Who's that?"

Quantrelle angled over to him, demanding, "Where does Doctor Elliott live?"

The sheriff came down to the sidewalk, peering up at him and saying, "Doc has already gone to Big T. You must of met him on the stageroad."

"I met a rig," Quantrelle said and got out of saddle. Then, as he tied his horse to the hitchrack, he asked abruptly, "How did Doc know he was needed at Big T?"

"I told him. Ike Gallatin rode in an hour ago, said Pat turned on him and that he shot in self defense."

"A goddam lie!" Quantrelle announced, and at this same instant, as batwing gates creaked across the plaza, turned to see Hal Barton come out of the saloon.

The Pool boss called, "Who was that rode in, George?" and now two other men came out behind him.

Quantrelle stood motionless, peering at those lamplit faces, identifying Gallatin and the mustached man he had seen step down from the Tombstone stage. Again, as he had that morning, Quantrelle sensed there was something familiar about the tall, stoop-shouldered man; as if he'd known the stranger at some time in the past.

"Who's over there with you?" Barton demanded.

Quantrelle moved away from Weaver. This, he understood was the beginning of trouble. Real trouble. The sheriff wouldn't do anything to avert it; Weaver would be thinking of his own hide — endeavoring to protect it at all costs. Quantrelle eased along the dark veranda until he came to its east end. Here he halted, and heard Weaver cross the veranda as Barton called arrogantly, "Speak up, George — speak up!"

Weaver hurried into the lobby, which reminded Quantrelle of what Apache Pat had said. George hadn't even waited to hear shooting before he ran off and hid . . .

Someone leaned out an upstairs window of the hotel, asking, "What's goin' on out there?"

And from across the plaza came Joe Pardee's voice, inquiring, "Who was that just rode in?"

"That's what I'm trying to find out," Barton declared. He said something to his companions and they fanned out, so that none of them were in the saloon's long shaft of lamplight as they came across the plaza.

Quantrelle thought now: *A hell of a place to be caught afoot.*

But he knew the bay didn't have a run left in him. Then he saw something across the plaza that brought a pleased grunt to his lips. He waited until he heard the dust-muffled tromp of oncoming boots, reckoned the nearest man was walking at an angle that would bring him some fifteen feet west of this spot. Then Quantrelle stepped into the street, moving slowly across the plaza, gun in hand and eyes probing the yonder darkness.

This, he understood, was cutting it awfully thin. If they discovered him now it would be three guns to one, with no escape. But he needed a fresh mount, and so he angled toward the saloon hitch rack where a buckskin horse stood barely visible on the fringe of doorway lamplight.

Gallatin's horse, Quantrelle guessed, and was within a dozen feet of it when someone lit a match across the plaza, and he heard Barton exclaim, "The Chisum branded bronc!"

Quantrelle smiled thinly, seeing this as a break in his favor. For now the yonder trio would concentrate on scouting that side of the street. They would think he was forted up between buildings over there; they might even go up to Sheriff Weaver's room, suspecting that he'd taken refuge with the badgetoter. Quantrelle stood motionless, listening for a long moment and hearing no sound of movement. Then he cat-footed toward the horse. If none of the trio turned around during these next few seconds he'd have time enough to get asaddle and make a run for it.

He was at the hitchrack, untying the buckskin's reins when he observed the fat-bellied barkeep in the saloon doorway. The man hadn't noticed him, his attention being strictly focused across the plaza. Quantrelle gathered up the reins. The rank smell of horse sweat came to him now, convincing him that this was Gallatin's horse. The animal had been recently ridden, but wouldn't be nearly as tired as the bay, for Gallatin had probably taken his time coming to town.

Quantrelle stepped quickly into saddle. He thought: *Now we make a run for it,* and felt a familiar sense of exuberance — the scalp tingling sensation of a gambler playing a poor hand for high stakes. And in this suspenseful moment heard the barkeep yell, "Over here — over here!"

Quantrelle fired a half-aimed shot at the saloon's front chandelier as he raced past, and missed, and heard the bullet shatter the backbar mirror. He was spurring his mount across the patch of lamplight when a slug smashed into the buckskin's head. The mortally wounded horse lunged on for a moment, then collapsed so suddenly that Quantrelle had no chance to jump clear. He went down with the buckskin, falling half under the somersaulting horse so that all the wind was knocked from his lungs by the force of impact.

Quantrelle gasped for air. Dust got into his nostrils and choked him. He was remotely aware of voices above him: Ike Gallatin saying, "He ain't hurt bad — yet."

Somebody struck a match and held it close to his face, its flame blinding him.

"That's him," Hal Barton announced. "That's Quantrelle!"

Then, as Quantrelle got up on one knee, still gasping for breath, something exploded along his forehead and there was neither sound nor feeling. There was nothing at all . . .

CHAPTER FOUR

Clay Quantrelle became aware of throbbing pain that pulsed at his temple, and an intolerable ache pounding his stomach. He opened his eyes, dimly seeing hoof-packed dust below him. The ground seemed to be moving and it made him dizzy to watch it. He retched, thoroughly nauseated. Presently he heard voices that were queerly garbled against the shuffling tromp of horses and the creak of saddles — voices that were near, yet above him, as if he were upside down.

"You shouldn't have pistol-whipped him," a man said. "Maybe you fractured his skull."

That sounded like Hal Barton's voice. But it was above Quantrelle and behind him somewhere, which seemed odd. Then, as he noticed a horse's hind legs moving methodically, Quantrelle realized that he was lying across a saddle, bound hand and foot.

"I owed him that tap on the noggin for

tellin' Tanner about me," Ike Gallatin muttered. "By God you damn near fixed my wagon for keeps, mistakin' Quantrelle for Shambrun like you did."

Shambrun!

That name was like a sharp spike prodding Quantrelle to full consciousness. He thought dazedly: So *that's why the stranger seemed familiar,* and understood at once why he hadn't recognized the gambler. Scarface Shambrun hadn't worn a mustache at Ellsworth. Dame Fortune, Quantrelle reflected, was up to her old tricks; of all the men she might have sent here, Shambrun had the most reason to hate him. And even more reason to hate Pat Tanner. Scarface could combine business with pleasure on this deal; he would take real satisfaction in seeing Barton smash Big T out of existence . . .

Quantrelle tried to alter the position of his body — to lessen the continuous pound of the saddle against his stomach. But he was lashed securely; and there was no way he could ease the constant jolting.

Hal Barton spoke again, saying, "We need Quantrelle alive. He's our scrapegoat, now that Tanner is out of it."

That puzzled Quantrelle. What did Barton mean by scrapegoat? For what? Why should the Rincon Basin Pool need a scapegoat? He was endeavoring to figure it out when he heard Shambrun's queerly falsetto voice: "What's the other payoff you mentioned, in case I don't take the thousand dollars?"

"A ten percent share of the profits," Barton said.

"What profits?"

Quantrelle listened eagerly, sharing Shambrun's curiosity in this — wanting to know how there could be profits to share. Range wars didn't end with profits; they ended with loss to all concerned.

"There's one big ranch and six small ones in Rincon Basin," Barton explained. "That's seven outfits, including mine. But at the finish there'll be just one big ranch — HB Connected. That's my brand. One big spread running from the Kettle Drums to the southern rim of Rincon Basin. Ike here will be my ramrod and own a twenty-five percent share of the whole shebang. If you want to gamble on a sure thing I'll give you a ten percent share — providing you stick through to the end with us."

The monstrousness of that declaration astonished Clay Quantrelle. It seemed so fantastic that he could scarcely believe he had heard it; thought this must be some senseless hallucination spawned by the punishment he'd taken. Such a scheme would involve elimination of Barton's partners in the Pool, including Jim Chalice; decimation of the very men who'd banded together to fight Pat Tanner's control of Rincon Basin. Could Barton actually be aiming toward such a goal?

As if in answer came Shambrun's question, "How about the other Pool members? What happens to them?"

Barton chuckled. "They'll go broke. In fact they're that way now, but I'm holding the Pool together."

"Out of the goodness of your big heart," Gallatin chuckled.

"What happens when the Pool goes out of business?" Shambrun inquired.

"I'll keep on fighting Big T," Barton explained. "I'll lend Jim Chalice enough to keep him from losing his place, because I'll own it eventually by marriage. But it wouldn't seem reasonable for me to keep lending money to all the others, so they'll just move out, owing me money. And when the thing is finished I take over their places by right of unpaid obligations."

Ike Gallatin laughed, said, "Nothin' could be simpler than that. There'll be no Pool at the windup. It's bankrupt now, and so is Tanner. It won't take much to put the whole caboodle out of business within a few weeks. Their cattle is scattered to hell and gone, thanks to me and Red Parmalee. Every time Red went callin' on Oley Swenson's gal he choused two-three head of Oley's steers toward the Bough on his way home."

"How about this Parmalee?" Shambrun asked. "Don't he figger in on our payoff?"

"Hell no," Gallatin scoffed. "Red had no idee I was in with Hal. He thought we was devilin' Pool members on Pat Tanner's account — just doin' an extra chore for Big T. Red wouldn't of met up with Swenson's gal in the first place if it wasn't for me sendin' him over there to chouse Oley's steers. After he met her Red took a real interest in his work."

Presently Hal Barton predicted, "Three good men can do the job at the windup. We won't need Pool members after we bust Tanner's beef gather."

Hearing all this, and understanding it now with stark clarity, Quantrelle felt a dismal sense of foreboding. Barton's fantastic scheme was rigged to destroy the Pool by pitting it against Big T, then he would finish the fight and build up a cattle empire from the wreckage of bankrupt ranches. The brutal viciousness of it — the sheer rapacity and lack of human decency — disgusted

Clay Quantrelle. Remembering Eve's fearful prediction of what would happen if Big T won the war, he thought: *She feared the wrong man.*

Ike Gallatin asked, "Does that sound big enough for you, Shambrun?"

"Yeah," the gambler agreed, his voice rising to falsetto laughter as he added, "It sounds dandy — if we win."

"Don't see how we can lose," Barton bragged. "I got the idea soon as I saw how Tanner was running things. Instead of taking it all for himself he just played at being a cow country king, electing sheriffs and telling folks what was best for them."

Presently the horses halted and Barton said, "Unload Quantrelle while I get the coffeepot going."

Quantrelle closed his eyes. There probably wasn't much chance of surviving this deal, but if Barton suspected his nefarious plans had been overheard there'd be no chance at all. A man who could plan so wanton a wipeout of neighbors wouldn't hesitate to kill an eavesdropper in cold blood . . .

Shambrun loosened the rope that bound Quantrelle's wrists, announcing, "He's still out cold."

Quantrelle allowed his hands to dangle limply, revealing no sign of the prickling sensation that needled them as renewed circulation drove the numbness from his fingers.

A hand was shoved against his shirt, feeling for heart beat, and now Ike Gallatin said, "He's alive. A swig of hot coffee spiked with likker will most likely fetch him around. I've saw 'em stay out for a whole day and then come to like nothin' had happened."

They lifted him off the horse and toted him into Barton's cabin where the appetizing aroma of boiling coffee came to Quantrelle.

"Set him in that corner," Barton ordered, "so we can pour a drink into him. He's liable to puke like a poisoned pup."

The coffee, when it came, was scalding hot. But it was a welcome excuse for Quantrelle to cease playing possum. He choked, and gagged, wanting this to seem real; he grunted and opened his eyes, blinking in dazed fashion and demanding, "What the hell is this?"

Hal Barton laughed. "You'll find out," he promised. "By God you'll find out plenty."

And Shambrun, who peered down at Quantrelle with a benevolent smile on his scarred, whisker-bristled face, asked, "Remember me, Quantrelle? Remember the last time we met, in Nauchville?"

Quantrelle nodded, warily alert and expecting a smash in the face. But the gambler merely laughed his high cackling laugh and said, "It's so nice to meet old friends. It is for a fact."

Then Hal Barton handed him a nearly full quart of whiskey, saying, "Take a swig for what ails you," and as if overcome by a sense of hospitality, the Pool boss brought him a fresh cup of coffee and a chunk of warmed-up beef.

Quantrelle was mildly surprised at such seeming kindness. For that, he understood, was all it amounted to — a false show of graciousness to throw him off guard. But why? What difference did it make to Barton what he thought? They had him trapped, unarmed, and half sick. What more did the Pool boss want? He watched Barton return to the table, wondering if the man was a trifle loco. Wondering too what Barton had meant about him being their scapegoat. Nothing that had happened since his arrival in Tailholt had made much sense, he thought grimly. It didn't seem possible that a man who'd had his fill of fighting should run into so much trouble while attempting to avoid it.

The hot coffee brought a welcome warmth to his aching, saddle-pounded stomach.

And it banished the dull throbbing in his head. Again he wondered why Barton had bothered to feed him, and could find no logical answer. But presently, as the three men finished their breakfast, Quantrelle understood what had prompted Barton's hospitality. For the Pool boss said, "You look like you're feeling good, Quantrelle — good enough to take the licking you're going to get."

Quantrelle stood up at once, knowing how this would be and deciding to delay it as long as possible. He watched Shambrun and Gallatin come at him from opposite sides while Barton stood directly in front of him; he thought dismally: *Three to one,* and knew there wasn't a chance to avoid the pooled punishment they so plainly planned. They had him with his back to a wall. Retreat was impossible.

Morning's first sunlight slanted in the cabin's east window now. But there was no cheerfulness in it for Clay Quantrelle. He shrugged, as if in surrender to the inevitable. His hands hung down, wrists showing the red marks of recent binding, and seemed utterly wilted — so demoralized that Hal Barton moved toward him confidently. Eagerly.

"You don't look so tough this morning,"

Barton taunted. "Not like you looked up there in the hotel room."

Quantrelle eyed him blankly, revealing no sign of tension tightened muscles. It was as if he were paralyzed by fear — by dread and awful expectancy. A wounded, terrified mouse of a man waiting for the cat-like pounce of his assailant.

"Yeller," Shambrun scoffed. "Yeller as calf manure."

And Gallatin said laughingly, "Sick as a gutted horse, by God."

Waiting until Barton was within two steps of him, Quantrelle drove forward so abruptly that Barton had no time to dodge the sledging right that landed flush on his blocky jaw. The thud of impact, the satisfaction of feeling Barton's flesh against his knuckles, and the sight of his confused backward dodging, stirred Quantrelle to sheer savagery. Rushing Barton he slammed him with both fists and shouted, "Now fight — you stinker!"

But before he could swing again his right arm was grasped by Shambrun who cackled, "Grab holt of him Ike — grab holt!"

Gallatin grasped his other arm and now they had him rigidly propped between them. Yet even so, knowing how hopeless further effort was, Quantrelle struggled desperately, using his boots against Shambrun's shins in an attempt to break loose.

Hal Barton gingerly rubbed his bruised jaw. "You'll pay, for that," he warned wrathfully. "By God you'll pay plenty!"

Quantrelle watched him move forward, waggling his right fist, hearing him mutter, "Now you get your needings."

"Brave, aren't you?" Quantrelle scoffed. "So goddam brave you need two helpers."

Barton laughed at him. Deliberately, as if taking time to savor the sadistic anticipation in him, Barton measured with his left, nudging Quantrelle's chin in the fashion of a photographer arranging a portrait poser to best advantage. Then he swung.

Quantrelle saw it coming. He tried to duck, but the fist caught him on the left nostril and cheek with an impact that knocked his head back against the log wall — that sent sharp splinters of bright light darting before his eyes.

"Dead centre!" Shambrun shrilled admiringly.

And then, as blood dribbled redly from Quantrelle's nose, Ike Gallatin said with mock concern, "Look what you went and done, Hal. He's bleedin'. The poor thing must be hurted."

A bland, satisfied smile creased Barton's

face now. But his eyes weren't smiling. They were coldly calculating, and colorless as new ice. The unblinking eyes of a rattlesnake, or of a mad man . . .

He stepped up to Quantrelle and using the heel of his hand, rubbed upward and around the bleeding nostril, spreading the blood so that it smeared Quantrelle's whole face. "You're blushing," he gloated. "You're blushing blood — you smart alecky bastard."

"Ain't he pretty," Shambrun chirped.

But Ike Gallatin was getting impatient. He said, "Hit him again, Hal. I like to see him squirm."

"Next one will be in the belly," Barton announced, and drove a jolting left to Quantrelle's midriff.

Quantrelle loosed a spasmodic grunt, and understood instantly that he should've held it back, for Barton said gleefully, "That made him squawk," and slammed another blow that seemed to crush the sore muscles of Quantrelle's saddle-bruised stomach.

"Squawk again!" Barton commanded arrogantly.

Quantrelle clamped his lips. He tried to roll with the blows that came, jolt on jolt; that turned him so sick he retched and lost part of the coffee. But he was being held

127

too tightly for more than a mere inch or two of movement. The gripping hands were like a vise, holding him helpless.

"Squawk, damn you — squawk!" Barton raged.

But Quantrelle took the punishment in stubborn silence and so the Pool boss transferred his attack, targeting Quantrelle's face with successive rights and lefts. Once, when Barton hit him squarely on the jaw, Quantrelle's knees buckled; whereupon Shambrun cautioned, "Not so hard, or you'll put him to sleep."

For a time then, Clay Quantrelle had no distinct knowledge of what was happening to him. He was remotely conscious of repeated blows that thudded against his face and body; of blood's warm wetness and its sweetish taste on his lips; of occasional scraps of talk and ribald laughter.

A dangling, endless nightmare of time that seemed to go on and on, so that it was repeating itself and he felt the same blows, over and over; heard the same taunting voices. The same chuckling laughter . . .

Finally, as if from a far distance, Quantrelle heard Barton say pantingly, "Give the son his horse and turn him loose."

"What for?" Shambrun demanded. "What you turnin' him loose for?"

"I told you he was our scapegoat, didn't I?" Barton demanded. "Now do like I say, damn it!"

Quantrelle felt himself being propelled across the yard. His eyes didn't seem to focus properly and he thought: *They're swelling shut.*

Free now, but so wobbly weak he could scarcely stand alone, Quantrelle leaned against the horse. He heard Gallatin order, "Climb up, smart boy — climb up."

Quantrelle found the horn, and grasped it, pulling himself into saddle. It was a slow, pain-prodded chore, and when he threw his right leg over the cantle he lost his balance and came so near to falling that Shambrun cackled, "Punch drunk as a beat up sheep-herder."

Abruptly then the horse was in motion and Quantrelle clung to the saddle's high fork with both hands, steadying himself against an increasing dizziness. It was, he thought vaguely, like riding in the dark and being drunk . . .

Eve Chalice was in the garden pulling up carrots when Fern Swenson rode up to the fence on her pinto pony and asked, "Have you seen any Big T riders go past this morning?"

"No," Eve said, and guessing which Big T rider Fern wanted to know about, added, "I haven't seen anything of Red Parmalee for several days."

Fern blushed. Scarcely past her seventeenth birthday she combined a girl's self-consciousness with the physical development of a woman. "I haven't seen him either," she admitted.

"Perhaps it would be better if you didn't," Eve suggested, for it was common gossip that her parents objected to Parmalee's courtship of their daughter. "It doesn't seem fitting for you to associate with a Tanner cowboy, Fern. Not now, when your father may have to fight Big T to protect his home."

"It's not my fault that Dad belongs to the Pool," Fern said, poutingly, "or that Red happens to work for Tanner."

The way she said it — as if there was nothing she could do about the matter — irritated Eve. "It isn't a question of fault, Fern. It's a matter of common sense. Your father can't welcome a Big T rider into his home, and he certainly won't like you meeting Red secretly out in the brush like a — a blanket squaw."

"Don't say that!" Fern exclaimed, her voice shrill with emotion. "Don't you dare

130

call me a blanket squaw!"

Eve eyed her in astonishment. "I didn't, Fern. I merely said how it would look to your parents. Red Parmalee is no school boy. He's five or six years older than you, and it's only natural that your folks don't approve of him."

"That doesn't make any difference when you're in love with a man," Fern said stubbornly.

"But you're not, really," Eve objected. "It's just a romantic friendship that can be broken if you'll look at it as a sensible girl should."

Fern shook her head. There was an expression of desperation in her eyes now — a wild, almost frantic expression. "It's too late for that," she said in a low, confessional voice, and looked down.

Eve didn't have to guess what she meant. It was plain to her now — so clear Eve wondered why she hadn't known it at once. "You poor child," she sympathized.

"I'm not a child," Fern protested. "I'm a woman. Even though you're older, I'm more of a woman than you are, Eve Chalice!"

Then, as if abruptly regretting what she had revealed, Fern whirled the pinto into a sharp turn. But halfway across the road she looked back, calling, "Next time Red rides past please ask him to come to see me, Eve. Say it's important."

"I will," Eve promised, and watching Fern ride off, thought how poor a choice of men she'd made. Red Parmalee had the flirty look of a man who'd laugh at matrimony, and shun any girl who suggested it.

"The poor kid," Eve murmured, and felt sorry for Fern's toil-worn folks. The Swensons were proud people; they fairly worshipped Fern, who was an only child.

As Eve stood there, moodily thinking about Fern's trouble, she saw a horseman come slowly along the road. At first she didn't recognize him; then, as he came near, she stared at Clay Quantrelle's bruised, blood-smeared face and demanded, "What in heaven's name happened to you?"

Quantrelle halted his horse. He peered at her through swollen eyes, as if not seeing her distinctly. Finally he said, "Hal Barton slugged me while two helpers held my arms."

"I don't believe it!" Eve exclaimed. "Hal wouldn't do such a cowardly, brutal thing!"

A grotesque grin quirked Quantrelle's battered lips. "I didn't expect you would," he muttered, gingerly fingering his raw, discolored face. "But it's so, regardless."

There was a flat, uncaring tone of truth to

his voice; as if it didn't make much difference whether she believed or not. That, and the slumped way he sat, like a man fighting to remain upright, convinced Eve. She crawled through the pine pole fence, and said soberly, "If Hal did that to you I'm ashamed of him."

Quantrelle didn't seem to hear her. He had taken out his Durham sack and was fumbling with a cigarette paper. When he poured the tobacco his aim was so poor that the flakes fluttered to the ground. He swore softly and tried again, tipping his head to peer at the paper. And missed again.

"Eyes must be crossed," he muttered. Discarding the paper he lifted the Durham sack toward his pocket and dropped it.

Eve picked up the tobacco. She placed it in his shirt pocket. "You'd better come to the house and let me doctor your face," she suggested.

The invitation seemed to surprise Quantrelle. He peered down at her as if doubting he had heard correctly. "Ears must be crossed also," he muttered.

"I'll lead your horse to the house," Eve offered, seeing how he gripped the saddle for support. She took the reins and walked up the path; glancing back and seeing that his eyes were closed, she warned, "Don't go to sleep."

"Just resting my eyes," Quantrelle mumbled.

Presently, as he got down in the cautious way of a man not quite drunk and not quite sober, he asked, "Is your father home?"

Eve shook her head, whereupon Quantrelle asked, "Aren't you taking a chance, ma'am — inviting a Big T stray into your house?"

"Dad would think so," Eve admitted. "He'd call me a nitwit." And remembering what she'd said to Fern Swenson, she added, "Perhaps I am."

Leading him into the parlor she pointed to her father's leather lounge and said, "Sit there until I fetch a pan of hot water."

"Gracias," Quantrelle said, easing onto the lounge with a gusty sigh.

Eve went to the kitchen, not quite sure why she was playing this angel-of-mercy role to an enemy of the Pool. Her father's enemy also. She frowned, recalling how primly she had advised Fern against association with Big T riders, and thought: *If Fern saw me now she'd think I'm a trifle touched in the head.* Eve tried to convince herself that she was doing this only because of Hal's surprising brutality. Then she wondered if she would have done the same thing for Red

Parmalee or Jim Jeddy; and knew she wouldn't. Which made her wonder the more . . .

When Eve went back to the parlor she found Clay Quantrelle stretched out, sound asleep. He looked boyish now. With his fist-scarred face and discolored eyes he looked like a tired kid sleeping; a bloody-nosed kid who'd been in a brawl and taken all the worst of it. A cowlick of shaggy black hair slanted down across his forehead; his battered face, so relaxed and somehow serene despite its bruises, revealed a refinement of feature she hadn't noticed before and she thought now: *He's better looking than I realized.*

Quantrelle lay unmoving as she bathed his face. He was still soundly sleeping when Eve's father rode into the yard near sundown and demanded, "What's that bay horse doin' in my corral?"

Hal Barton had been asaddle most of the day, making his rounds. Late in the afternoon he rode up to Oley Swenson's ramshackle place to find the old man sitting moodily on his front stoop.

"I've got some good news," Barton announced smilingly.

Swenson grunted a wordless greeting. He

135

looked, Barton thought, like a man weighted by more worry than he knew how to handle . . .

"We've got Ike Gallatin on our side now," Barton reported. "He's all through at Big T."

That news visibly impressed Swenson. "How come?" he demanded.

"Ike didn't want Tanner to hire that drifter, Quantrelle. They got into a jangle and Tanner grabbed for his gun. Ike shot him and rode off. He came over to my place and gave me some interesting news, Oley — real interesting news indeed."

Fern Swenson came around from the kitchen doorway and asked, "Will you take potluck with us, Mr. Barton?"

"No thank you, ma'am," Barton said, bowing with a habitual gallantry toward women.

"Mae says we'd be pleasured to have you stay for supper."

"Express my regrets to her," Barton said, blandly smiling. "Nothing would please me more, but I have important business in town this evening."

When the girl went back to the kitchen, Barton motioned for Swenson to follow him toward the corral. "Don't want the women folks to hear what I'm saying," he explained.

"Why not?" Swenson asked, following him.

Barton shrugged, said slyly, "Well, from what I've heard, your girl is somewhat friendly with one of Tanner's riders."

"Who told you that?"

"Gallatin. Ike says Red Parmalee did considerable nightriding in this direction."

Oley Swenson scowled. "No business of his," he muttered. Then he asked, "How bad is Tanner hurt?"

"Bad enough to keep him bedfast for a spell. Ike says the old hellion is broke. Tanner didn't have enough cash to properly provision his chuckwagon for the early beef-gather he's planning to make. Ike says Tanner's only chance of staying in business is to market a big bunch of steers in Benson by next week. Which means the Pool must stop him from doing it."

Barton let that sink in, then added, "There's to be a meeting at my place tomorrow afternoon. I've called on Mike Halloran, Bill Peeble and Gus Anderson today, telling them to be there. We've got to get ready for action right away."

"What kind of action?" Swenson asked.

Barton tapped his holster. "Gun action," he said quietly. "The only kind that can stop Big T from gathering a trail herd."

Swenson didn't like that and showed it in the way he asked, "You mean we bust up the gather by shooting at Big T riders?"

Barton nodded, asked, "How else could it be done?"

"What do the others say about that?"

"They're for it a hundred percent," Barton lied. "They want to see Big T busted, once and for all. This is our chance, Oley — the best chance we'll ever have to put the Pool on top where it belongs. Instead of Tanner calling the turn, we'll call it, and fence the ranch as we see fit. But first we've got to stop that beef gather."

Swenson slowly shook his head. "Jim Chalice won't be for it," he said, voicing a judgment born of long association with Cross Crescent's owner. "Jim won't think it's fitting for us to attack a roundup crew that's handlin' their own cattle."

Barton frowned. He had heard similar reasoning on three previous occasions today, and was heartily sick of it. Every Pool member he'd talked to had asked how Jim Chalice felt — as if Eve's father was running the Pool. It was enough to make a man sorry he'd ever got mixed up with a warm-eyed woman. If it wasn't for Eve he could say what he thought about Jim Chalice . . .

Using an established argument, Barton

said patiently, "We have no choice, Oley. Look what Tanner has done to us already. Burned our shipment of wire, choused our cattle into the roughs. And there'll be worse to come, if he stays in business. We can't get any protection from our mealy-mouthed sheriff, so it's up to us to protect ourselves. And there's just one way to do that, no matter how rough it seems."

"I still don't like it," Swenson said. "And neither will Jim Chalice."

Irritation got the best of Hal Barton. "You'd better like it," he warned. "You'd better go along with the rest of us."

Then, in a more gracious tone, he added, "Regardless of how Jim feels about it, he'll do what the majority decides. You can bank on that."

"No," Swenson said stubbornly. "Jim will do what he thinks best, regardless of what others do. And so will I."

Whereupon he turned and walked to the house.

Quantrelle awoke to the sound of voices, and a lamplit room that was strange to him — until he saw Eve Chalice standing near the front doorway with her father. Then, understanding where he was, he recalled Eve's gracious invitation, and thought: *I must've fallen asleep.* Embarrassed by that knowledge, Quantrelle swung off the lounge at once, wincing at the soreness of his stomach muscles; he was standing when Eve introduced him to her father.

Jim Chalice made no move to shake hands. His voice was barely civil as he said, "Howdy," and went on out to the veranda.

Eve nodded toward the kitchen, saying, "I saved some supper for you."

"Supper?" Quantrelle mused, a self-mocking smile slanting his bruised cheeks. "You mean that on top of everything else, you're going to feed me, ma'am?"

"Of course," she said cheerfully. "Cross Crescent always feeds stray riders who are hungry. Especially those that look as if they'd been drug through a knothole by the heels."

Watching as she moved about the stove, Quantrelle admired the sweet, soft line of her gently smiling lips and the womanly, apron-draped shape of her. He had liked her better each time they met; it occurred to him now that she possessed an impelling attraction regardless of what she wore or where he saw her. When she loaded his plate with beef and frijoles the feminine scent of her hair was like an intimate perfume, well remembered.

"How do you feel?" she inquired.

"Better than I look, most likely," Quantrelle said. Remembering that Barton had deliberately smeared his face with blood, he added, "I must've been a gory mess before you washed my face."

Even though he was ravenously hungry, Quantrelle couldn't keep his eyes off her. This was the way a man should live, with a woman to serve him supper when the day's riding was done — a young, sweet-smelling woman who could make a man forget his troubles. Contemplating his hostess as she refilled his coffee cup, Quantrelle decided that he had never known a more gracious woman, nor one more desirable.

Eve sat at the table, seeming to take satisfaction in watching him eat with such thorough relish. Presently she said, "Dad had an argument with Red Parmalee today while he was chousing a couple of our strays off Big T range. Red treated Dad as if he was some greasy-sack nester who'd steal the saddle off a horse. I guess that's why Dad acted so unsociable toward you."

The reference to Red Parmalee was like a cold wind entering this cheerful room. It reminded Quantrelle how odd it was for him, a Big T rider, to be here; and how ridiculous his romantic notions were. For this warm-eyed woman believed the fight against Pat Tanner was a crusade of survival for her father and his friends. She had no way of knowing that they were marked for ruin by the very man who led them. The man whose ring she had accepted . . .

"A penny for your thoughts," Eve offered.

Quantrelle shrugged. "I doubt if you'd consider them worth a penny."

"I might," she suggested. "I'm especially fond of thoughts."

Quantrelle shaped up a smoke, wondering if she would believe him if he told her what he'd overheard at daybreak this morning. Barton's scheme was so vicious that it might sound utterly fantastic to Eve. And to her father. Yet even so, half expecting she might laugh at him, Quantrelle decided to tell her. He thought: *I owe her that much and more.* He was on the verge of speaking when it occurred to him that revealment of Barton's scheme might be dangerous — to her. In the event Eve and her father doubted the story, they might tell Barton about it as a matter of loyalty, or of allowing him a chance to deny it. In either case they would reveal possession of information which the Pool boss would want suppressed — at any price.

"Well?" Eve prompted.

142

"Changed my mind," Quantrelle said.

"I thought only women were allowed that privilege," Eve censured. And then, as her father came charging into the kitchen, she demanded, "What's wrong?"

"Big T riders are pullin' down our garden fence," Chalice announced, reaching for a Winchester above the kitchen door. He peered at Quantrelle's empty holster and said gruffly, "You keep away from me, mister — clear away."

As the old cowman limped hurriedly outside, Eve called, "Be careful, Dad — please be careful!"

Quantrelle reached for the lamp and blew it out and said, "You'd better put out the parlor lamp also."

Chalice was firing now, the Winchester making methodically spaced explosions out in the yard. Then other guns opened up from the road and Quantrelle muttered, "The damn fools!"

This, he supposed, was the crew's way of striking back at the Pool for Apache Pat's shooting. But they were picking on the wrong man. "The crazy damn fools," he whispered, and felt his way into the parlor.

Eve had blown out the lamp. Quantrelle found her near the front doorway, peering at yellow blooms of muzzle flame that flared briefly out by the road. "Is there another gun here?" he asked.

"What difference would it make?" she asked, her throaty voice revealing the high excitement in her. "They're your friends, aren't they?"

Which was a pair of questions Clay Quantrelle couldn't answer, nor explain exactly why he'd asked about the gun. Surely he couldn't shoot at Big T riders. Yet this night attack against a man's home was entirely unwarranted; it violated the very fundamentals of justice and decency.

A bullet smashed a front window, coming in at an angle that carried it directly above Eve's head before it hit the room's side wall. Quantrelle grasped her by the shoulders, propelling her into the kitchen and saying, "You stay here."

Then he stepped outside.

Jim Chalice was reloading his gun behind the windmill water trough. He said nervously, "Stay back, Quantrelle," and levered a fresh shell into the firing chamber.

The yonder firing had ceased also, and now Quantrelle said, "I'm going to walk out there, if you'll quit firing so they'll recognize my voice when I yell at them."

"They'll probably take a shot at you," Chalice warned. "Those drunken bums don't care who they shoot at."

"I'll take the chance," Quantrelle muttered. He was passing the water trough when he heard a hoot of jeering laughter and the hoofpound of horses galloping off toward the Big T fork.

"They've done their damage," Chalice muttered wrathfully. He stood silent for a moment, listening to the fading hoof tromp. Then he said, "Go saddle your horse, Quantrelle. And when you get to Big T tell Tanner this raidin' business works both ways."

"Apache Pat had nothing to do with it," Quantrelle said. "Ike Gallatin shot Pat last night."

"Gallatin shot him!" Chalice echoed. "What are you talkin' about?"

"Ike was the Pool's spy at Big T," Quantrelle explained. "Pat found it out."

"That's loco!" Chalice exclaimed. "Pure loco!"

Quantrelle shrugged, knowing how useless it would be to try convincing this man, or his daughter. The Hal Barton they knew was a totally different person from the sadistic devil who'd beaten a held man this morning. They saw him as an energetic, courteous, right-minded man who had the interest of his neighbors at heart — a handsome, blandly smiling man with the gumption to fight for his principles.

"The Pool has no spies," Chalice said. "We've scarcely got money enough to buy cartridges, to say nothing of hiring spies. You tell Tanner I ain't forgetting what happened tonight. My boy will be home soon and then there'll be two Chalice guns against Big T."

No, Quantrelle thought, watching Chalice limp away: there'd never be two of them. Bob's gun had fired its final shot in Tombstone. It was an odd thing. For the first time now, Quantrelle hated the man he had killed in the Crystal Palace — the tough-faced fool who had unwittingly propelled him into this Judas role in Rincon Basin. Gone now was the awful sense of guilt; in its place was profound conviction that Bob Chalice had cheated him out of the only woman he'd ever wanted.

"Damn him," Quantrelle muttered. "Damn him to hell."

He was in the dark corral, endeavoring to catch the bay, when Eve came out with a lantern. She asked, "Now do you understand why the Pool has to win?"

Quantrelle shook his head. "I understand that all range wars are bad, no matter who fights them," he said, and bridled his horse.

"But don't you think we are right?" Eve insisted. "Doesn't what you've seen here prove that?"

Quantrelle lifted his saddle from the kak pole. "Pat Tanner," he admitted, "may be partly to blame. He's stubborn and brash in his habits. But Hal Barton is responsible for this trouble. He's the only man who'll win anything, and there'll be no peace in this country while he lives."

"Why Clay — how can you say such a thing?" Eve demanded. She held the lantern so that it lighted his face, and now she said in a queerly pleased voice, "I believe you are jealous."

Quantrelle gave his attention to saddling the bay. He thought: *She's partly right,* and was surprised that she had so accurately judged him.

"I didn't think you were that romantic," Eve teased.

Quantrelle ignored her. He pulled up the cinch, not speaking until it was properly adjusted. Then he said, "Thanks for your fine hospitality, Eve."

"You're very welcome," she said. The gravity of her thinking now was reflected in her voice and in her lantern-lit eyes; it was an increasing pressure that brought a frown to her smooth cheeks. "It doesn't seem right

147

or fitting that you should fight against my father, Clay. He's an honest, God-fearing man, and you're a —"

"A drifter who has to pay a debt," Quantrelle offered.

A humorless, cynical smile altered the soft curve of Eve's lips. "My brother is a drifter, also, Clay. He's coming home to pay a debt of loyalty to his father. And you'll be shooting at him, if you fight against the Pool."

"I don't think so," Quantrelle muttered. "I don't think your brother will come home."

"Oh yes he will," Eve insisted. "We received a letter from him yesterday. He'll be here within a week."

Quantrelle peered at her in narrow-eyed wonderment. He asked, "Is your brother's name Bob?"

She nodded, said defensively, "He'd have been home already, except for a misfortune in Texas."

Her brother had had a misfortune all right, Quantrelle reflected grimly; but it was in Arizona — not Texas. The letter must've been delayed considerably in transit, he supposed . . .

"Bob was robbed, and hurt so badly that he spent three weeks in a hospital," Eve explained. "It's a wonder he's alive."

Slowly, in the dazed fashion of a man overwhelmed by news so good he scarcely dared believe it, Quantrelle asked, "Did he mention losing a moneybelt?"

"Yes — with almost two hundred dollars in it."

Quantrelle loosed a gusty sigh. He thought: *So I killed the man who robbed Bob Chalice!*

"Do you know my brother?" Eve asked wonderingly.

"No — but I like him," Quantrelle said, very sober about this. "I like him a lot."

And now, seeing this as another of Dame Fortune's trifling tricks, he laughed for the first time in months . . .

"What's so comical?" Eve inquired, completely puzzled.

"Life," Quantrelle told her. "God's joke on the human race."

That made no sense to her, and now, as Jim Chalice called, "It's past bedtime, Eve," and slammed the kitchen door behind him, she stepped close to Quantrelle. "Won't anything make you change your mind about fighting the Pool?"

She was so close that the fragrance of her breeze-ruffled hair strongly affected him. He said, "No," intending to step into saddle — to show her that no sweet-smelling woman could have her way with him. But instead he took her in his arms.

"Eve!" he whispered, pulling her hard against him — feeling the cushioned pressure of her woman's body as he had that first day in town.

She still clung to the lantern. "Clay, you musn't," she objected, and used her free hand to push him back.

But there was an impelling urge in Clay Quantrelle now; an overwhelming desire so elemental that he could scarcely resist it. Yet even so, with the thrusting need of her pulsing through him, Quantrelle said, "Give me one kiss to remember, Eve. That's all I'm asking — just something to remember."

And then he kissed her in the hungry fashion of a man long famished.

Eve dropped the lantern. Both her arms tightened about his shoulders and her lips made a merging pressure against his lips. For a timeless interval while the woman sweetness of her rocked all his senses, Quantrelle held her hard against him. Until she used her hands to push away from him, saying breathlessly, "No, Clay — no!"

Jim Chalice came out to the kitchen stoop. He called, "What's going on?"

"I'll be right in," Eve promised, stepping away from Quantrelle. She picked up the lantern, saying softly, "Good night."

Quantrelle got into saddle. He said, "I'm not fighting against your father, Eve. I'm fighting against Hal Barton. Maybe you'll understand why — later on."

Then he rode out of the yard, watching over his shoulder as Eve toted the lantern back to the house.

CHAPTER FIVE

The smell of recently disturbed dust made a plain taint in the air as Quantrelle followed the road to Lookout Ridge. He judged that not more than two or three riders had raided the Cross Crescent fence. Red Parmalee, he supposed, recalling what Eve had told him about her father's argument with the redhead; and Kid Calhoun, or Sonora. Jim Jeddy would stick close to Apache Pat, wanting to protect him from another sneak attack.

Tonight's foolish fence-busting would probably stir up a reprisal raid from Pool members. It meant the shooting might start before another day had passed. But even so, with that trouble impending and the fretful realization that he must arrange a marriage for Fern Swenson, Quantrelle rode northward with a grin on his face. Bob Chalice was alive, and Bob's sister was the most kissable woman west of the Pecos.

"East or west," Quantrelle mused, remembering how it had been with her in his arms. It made a man itch, just thinking about it . . .

Eve was wearing Barton's ring, but that hadn't kept her from hugging a Big T rider, nor from responding to his kiss. It occurred to Quantrelle now that Eve might have been endeavoring to win his loyalty away from Apache Pat; recalling how she'd asked, "Won't anything keep you from fighting against the Pool," he wondered if that was her only reason for permitting such intimacy.

Quantrelle was thinking about that when he was challenged on the ridge by Kid Calhoun who asked, "What was all that shootin' I heard off towards Cross Crescent?"

The question surprised Quantrelle. "Didn't some of our crew just pass here?" he demanded.

"No," the Kid said. "Nobody passed here all evenin'. But I heard riders down below there in the timber a little bit ago."

Instantly then Quantrelle understood that the raiders hadn't been members of Tanner's crew; they'd been Barton, Shambrun and Gallatin!

"A fake raid," he muttered, "for the purpose of making Jim Chalice mad enough to fight."

"What do you mean by that?" Calhoun asked.

But Quantrelle ignored the question. He was thinking how close he had come to walking into sure slaughter back there at Cross Crescent. Except for a matter of moments in timing he would have been a blundering target that wouldn't have been missed. Dame Fortune, he decided, had taken a real fancy to him this night. The slutty wench had her arms around him . . .

He asked, "How's Apache Pat?"

"Doc says he's goin' to make it. The bullet busted a rib and glanced off."

"Good!" Quantrelle exclaimed, thoroughly pleased. As he rode on across the ridge, Kid Calhoun called, "You reckon them riders I heard are fixin' for trouble tonight?"

"I doubt it," Quantrelle counselled, "but keep your eyes peeled, Kid. No telling what Barton's bunch will do."

Riding down the steep, switch-back trail onto the mesa, he contemplated Barton's night-riding trick, seeing the sly strategy of it, and understanding that it would rouse Pool members to a showdown fight that might wreck both the Pool and Big T before another week had passed. As of tonight, Hal Barton held all the aces.

Sheriff Weaver came off the front gallery and walked with Quantrelle to the corral, saying, "I should of given you a hand last night, but by the time I came down from my room you was gone."

It was, Quantrelle supposed, a coward's way of apologizing for his cowardice. George Weaver would never give anyone a hand if the giving meant risk to his own hide . . .

"Where'd you go?" Weaver inquired.

Quantrelle grinned, unsaddling his horse. George was real curious now, but last night there'd been no curiosity in him at all — when it might have done some good. "I took a little ride over toward Barton's place," he said.

"What for?" Weaver asked, wholly puzzled.

"Just for the fun of it," Quantrelle said cynically. "It was a nice night for riding and there was nothing else to do."

Then he crossed the yard and went in to see Apache Pat.

The old cowman lay propped on pillows, his wrinkled face looking like bleached saddle leather in the lamplight. "Where the hell you been?" he demanded, and when Quantrelle grinned down at him, Tanner asked, "What happened to your face?"

"Fell off my horse," Quantrelle lied, seeing no reason to worry a crippled old man

155

with gory details. "What do we do now, Pat?"

"Start the beef gather," Tanner said impatiently. "I want you to ramrod the crew and git at it. Gramp can take care of me, and Weaver will stay around, not that he'd make much difference in a pinch. But he's got a gun. Sonora can do the cookin' for you boys while you're out with the wagon."

"Wouldn't it look better if you made Jim Jeddy roundup boss?" Quantrelle asked. "He knows the country. I don't."

Apache Pat shook his head. "I want a driver, and Jim ain't no driver. He's too goddam easy-goin'. I've got to git a trail herd gathered while the gittin' is good. Barton's bunch ain't goin' to sit on their tails much longer."

"All right," Quantrelle said, "but I've got an errand to do in town tomorrow. We'll start our gather Sunday."

"What kind of a errand?" Tanner demanded, plainly displeased.

Quantrelle shrugged, said, "A friend of mine is getting married."

Tanner eyed him in astonishment. Exasperation brought a stain of color to his pale cheeks and he demanded, "You mean you're lettin' a goddam weddin' interfere with our beef gather?"

"I made a promise, and I'm keeping it," Quantrelle said quietly.

Tanner lay back on the pillows with a sighing curse. "Never saw the beat of it," he complained. "Seems like every goddam thing in the world gits in the way of my roundup. But I never supposed you'd go social on me, by God — I never figgered you was that kind of galoot."

Gramp Pettigrue came in from the kitchen with a pot of coffee. "You ain't supposed to rant and rave like a drunk sheepherder," he complained. "Doc said for you to lay quiet, and git back your strength."

"Strength hell!" Tanner fumed. "I'm stronger right now than you've ever been. To hear you talk anybody'd think I'd been gutshot!"

Quantrelle grinned. Gramp would have his hands full trying to control this wild old rannyhan. Apache Pat had lost a lot of blood in addition to suffering a broken rib, but his arrogance hadn't been dented at all. Now Quantrelle asked, "Is there a spare six-gun around here I can borrow?"

Tanner motioned toward a pair of Colt forty-fives that hung on the wall. "Take one of them," he directed. He eyed Quantrelle narrowly, adding, "I suppose you lost your gun when you fell off the horse and hurt your face."

"Yeah," Quantrelle agreed. He slipped the gun into holster and went on out to the gallery where Sheriff Weaver sat smoking a cigar.

"I wouldn't put it past Ike Gallatin to make another try at killin' Pat," George said worriedly. "That galoot is plain hazardous."

"Don't reckon he'd try it by himself again," Quantrelle predicted. "Ike knows we'll be watching for him. But I wish there was some way to keep Jim Chalice and his friends from committing suicide, which is what this thing will be for them when the showdown comes."

"Only way they could be kept from fightin' would be to handcuff 'em," Weaver said pessimistically. "Hal Barton has 'em so worked up they can't think straight. I met Bill Peeble on the way in this afternoon. He says there's to be a Pool meetin' tomorrow afternoon at Barton's place — to make plans for a real fight against Big T."

The Pool boss had the stage all set, Quantrelle reflected. That fake raid on Cross Crescent tonight would be the spark to ignite them — to set them at Big T in a dog-eat-dog fight. Barton was a master at slick conniving. No wonder he had so thoroughly deceived the Chalices . . .

"You startin' the beef gather tomorrow?" Weaver asked, as Quantrelle headed toward the bunkhouse.

"Sunday," Quantrelle told him, and thinking of the chore he had to accomplish tomorrow, thought: *A different kind of gather.* Red, he supposed would be highly indignant — might even choose to fight it out. He was wondering about that as he went into the bunkhouse and heard the loud snores of three sleeping men. No matter how the deal went, Red wouldn't be sleeping here tomorrow night.

His promise to Oley Swenson was the last thing Quantrelle thought about before he went to sleep, and the first thing that came back to his mind the next morning. Watching Parmalee at the breakfast table, Quantrelle gave the redhead a thoughtful attention. It was a custom long established, this appraisal of another man's caliber; it had paid dividends in the past. Red, he decided, was no professional gunslinger; just a rough, tough cowboy who might be a fair hand at fighting. But there was no telling what a man might do in anger.

I'll soon know, Quantrelle thought. Presently, as they left the kitchen, he moved in beside Parmalee and said, "Let's go over to the corral for a little talk."

Red went with him, asking, "What's up?"

"A private matter," Quantrelle said, and when they reached the corral fence, he announced, "I promised Swenson that you'd marry his daughter within three days."

"*You* promised!" Red blurted.

Quantrelle nodded, meeting Parmalee's anger-flared eyes directly. "This is the third day."

"But what goddam right you got making a promise like that?"

A whimsical smile creased Quantrelle's cheeks. "Just a case of human nature," he explained in a casual tone of voice. "Most men have one queer streak in them, Red. Some dislike pinto horses, others don't like dogs. I knew a man once that didn't like whiskey, and he was a Texan to boot. Well, my queer streak is a dislike for men who get young women in trouble and run out on them."

Observing the confused — almost dumbfounded — expression in Parmalee's eyes, Quantrelle thought: *He figures I've gone haywire in my head.*

"Suppose I say to hell with your queer streak?" Red demanded.

Quantrelle looked him in the eye for a moment, then asked, "Can you outdraw me?"

Parmalee's freckled face went slack-jawed

160

with astonishment. "You mean a head-to-head shootout?"

Quantrelle nodded.

Red peered at him as if disbelieving what he saw and heard. Finally he demanded, "What's Fern Swenson to you?"

"Just a girl I met once, in the moonlight," Quantrelle said. "A worried girl sitting on a pinto horse with her skirts hiked up so that her legs showed. She has nice legs, Red — real nice."

"By God you must be loco," Parmalee muttered.

"And fairly fast with a gun," Quantrelle agreed. As if wanting to be perfectly fair about this, he said, "Chances are I'd only break your right arm, Red. Above the elbow most likely. I wouldn't aim to kill you."

And seeing the involuntary way Parmalee glanced at his arm, Quantrelle felt a secret amusement. Men like Red couldn't comprehend death, which was a mysterious unreality. But a broken bone was very real to him. A thing to be dreaded . . .

"Then I'd give you another chance to do right by Fern Swenson," Quantrelle resumed. "Even a one-armed husband is better than none, when there's a baby on the way."

"Suppose I still said no?"

Quantrelle shrugged. "A sensible man wouldn't be that stubborn, Red. But if he was, there'd still be a left arm to break."

He gave Parmalee time to absorb that, then asked, "Why be so mule mean about it, Red. I'm not saying you've got to live with the girl forever. Just long enough to make it look right. All you have to do is make things easy for Fern, and her folks — and for yourself. I'll even pay the preacher, and rent you a room at the Belvedere for your wedding night."

"That would be somethin'," Parmalee mused, "to have Fern in a hotel room all night." A slow grin creased his freckled cheeks as he thought about it. "She's a fine girl, Fern. I never figgered on marryin', but a man could do a lot worse."

"She'd be real nice to come home to of an evening," Quantrelle said.

"Yeah," Red muttered, "but I got no home."

"Apache Pat might let you have a room in the house," Quantrelle suggested. Then a new thought struck him; "Fern could take care of Pat while we're on roundup, instead of Gramp Pettigrue!"

"Hell yes!" Red agreed enthusiastically, "And Gramp could cook for us. I'd hate like hell to eat Sonora's cookin' for a whole

162

week. He ain't fit to slop hogs."

Quantrelle laughed. This deal, which had seemed tragic last night, was turning out even better than he'd dared hope it would. "Your marriage to Fern will benefit the whole outfit," he said. "It sure as hell will."

Fern Swenson was helping her mother prepare a batch of corn bread when her father came into the kitchen. "Red Parmalee is out at the barn," he announced. "Says he wants to see you."

Astonishment had its way with Fern. Her face turned pale. She stared at her father as if fearing this was some sort of joke. "You mean — Red is out there now?" she demanded.

Swenson nodded. "Don't just stand there like a nitwit," he said censuringly. "You've got to learn not to keep a man waitin'."

Fern hurried out then, wiping flour-dusted hands on her apron. But when she reached the yard and saw Red waiting she slowed to a more casual approach, not wanting to appear overly eager.

Red took off his hat, revealing carrot-colored hair sleeked down with pomade. "Hello, honey," he greeted.

Fern ran to him. "Red," she cried, "oh Red!"

Watching this at the kitchen window, Mrs. Swenson smiled. A warm glow came to her faded eyes and she said, "Mister Parmalee is wearing his Sunday suit. Looks real nice in it."

"I still don't understand how that man Quantrelle did this," Oley said, slowly shaking his head.

"We will not question the workings of God's will," Mrs. Swenson murmured, quite content.

Presently, as Fern and Red came toward the house, she turned to her sober-faced husband saying, "We must let bygones be bygones, Oley."

She walked over and patted his arm and whispered, "You were not so strictly proper sometimes, when the courting fever was in you. Remember?"

Fern brought Red into the kitchen, a radiant smile on her flushed face. "We are to be married in town this afternoon!" she announced. "Red has to go on roundup tomorrow morning."

"It is well," Mrs. Swenson said. She motioned to the table, inviting, "Have a cup of coffee, Red. Also a piece of apple pie."

"Don't mind if I do," Parmalee said. "That's my favorite kind of pie."

Oley Swenson went into the bedroom. "I

shall wear my Sunday suit also," he announced and closed the door.

Clay Quantrelle and Jim Jeddy sat their horses at the fringe of timber just west of Swenson's homestead. They had observed Red's meeting with Fern in the yard, and now Jeddy mused, "He sure had me fooled complete. From the way Red talked about wimmin' you'd figger he was a parlor house sport and not a marryin' man at all."

"Men change sudden, sometimes," Quantrelle said. He grinned, thinking how he'd given Red the last of his meager funds to finance a one-night honeymoon.

As Parmalee and the girl went into the house, Jeddy muttered, "This'll sort of complicate things, won't it? Havin' a Big T man married to the daughter of a Pool member sort of makes us all shirt tail relations."

Quantrelle nodded. But his thoughts were on another chore. The idea of paying Hal Barton a visit had come to him this morning as he eyed the reflection of his battered face in the bunkhouse mirror. Now, with his promise to Oley Swenson about to be fulfilled, an increasing impatience nagged him.

"Can we reach Barton's place before

noon?" he asked.

"A trifle sooner, by goin' cross country instead of by the road," Jeddy said, then added in a mildly disapproving voice, "Beatin' up Hal Barton won't git you nothin' but sore knuckles. What he needs is a bullet."

Quantrelle shrugged. No use endeavoring to make Jim Jeddy understand why he had to punish Barton with his fists. Jim was strictly a gun fighter. The bald-headed little rider had probably never hit a man in his life, or been hit — by a fist.

"Looks like the whole family is goin' to town," Jeddy remarked, watching the women folks wait on the stoop while Swenson and Red hooked a team to the buckboard. "Red acts like a married man already."

Quantrelle watched Swenson drive out of the yard with his wife and daughter sharing the high spring seat while Parmalee rode alongside the rig, his Sunday hat tilted at a jaunty angle.

"That shows you how romantic fever can hit a man when he least expects it," Jeddy mused. "Red must of got it real bad."

"Let's ride," Quantrelle suggested, and there was an increasing eagerness in him as he followed Jeddy southward. This deal seemed like rank foolishness to Jim, but it might prove something which needed proving — that Hal Barton wasn't much of a man in a fair fight. That possibility, combined with a prodding itch for revenge, stirred a stronger and stronger sense of anticipation in Quantrelle. The supposition that Gallatin and Shambrun would be at Barton's place and thus make the odds three-to-two, didn't seem important. According to Jeddy it wouldn't be difficult to take the place by surprise. With cautious maneuvering and a little luck they should ride into the yard from the back without being seen . . .

They did, Quantrelle easing his horse along the west side of the log house while Jeddy came around the barn. Hal Barton and Shambrun were roosting on the corral fence, watching Ike Gallatin shoe a horse. All three had their backs to Quantrelle when he called sharply, "Reach, you bastards!"

Hal Barton's head snapped around as if yanked by an invisible rope. "What the hell!" he exclaimed, staring at Quantrelle's leveled gun. He was unarmed, but Shambrun was wearing his gungear and his right hand was hidden by the turn of his body.

"I said reach!" Quantrelle commanded, his voice harsh with hatred.

Shambrun lifted his right hand shoulder high and held it there while Jim Jeddy rode up to him, taking his gun and tossing it across the corral. Then the little rider looked at Ike Gallatin who stood with a horseshoe in one hand and a hammer in the other.

"Come on out," Jeddy invited with habitual mildness.

"What you figgerin' to do?" Gallatin asked.

Jeddy eared back the hammer of his gun, the cocking mechanism making a clicking sound against the yard's quiet silence. "You want to walk out, or be drug out by the boots?" Jeddy asked, not raising his voice.

As Jeddy came toward the gate, Hal Barton got down from the fence and faced Quantrelle. "What's the meaning of this?" he demanded.

Quantrelle ignored the question, guessing that Barton was worried, and wanting him to worry. He watched Gallatin come out of the corral with hands held shoulder high. Big T's ex-ramrod was worried also, Quantrelle saw, and so was Shambrun. They were wondering if this was to be a lynching or a massacre . . .

"Hand me up your gun," Jeddy said to Gallatin, then added, "Butt first, unless you'd like to try a little fancy shootin'

168

betwixt us two."

Ike looked into the muzzle of Jeddy's gun. "You think I'm loco?" he muttered, and used his left hand to bring the gun out.

"I think you're a snaky sneak," Jeddy said quietly, and now, as Gallatin reached up to hand over the gun, Jim slashed down, pistol-whipping Ike's extended arm between wrist and elbow. Hard.

The plain sound of a bone breaking was echoed by Gallatin's yelp of pain. He dropped the gun and gripped his broken arm, holding it tight against his belly. "You broke it!" he accused in an outraged voice. "By God you broke my arm!"

"That's for what you done to Apache Pat," Jeddy said, showing no anger, even now. "It should've been your right one, though." He glanced at Quantrelle, asking, "Shall I bust his other arm also, Clay?"

Quantrelle shook his head, wholly astonished at this calm brutality. Despite his seeming meekness, Jim was a deep and merciless hater — a strict disciple of the Indian code of an eye for an eye . . .

"Keep watch on the spectators," Quantrelle said, "while I give Mister Barton a lesson in head-to-head slugging."

"So that's it," Barton said, his voice plainly showing the relief he felt; showing

169

too a returning arrogance as he scoffed, "You talk tough against an unarmed man."

"Like you did, the first time we met," Quantrelle reminded.

He dismounted, unbuckled his gungear and hung it on the saddlehorn. Then he said, "Come on, pretty boy. Let's see you fight."

"Sure," Barton agreed. But he didn't seem overly confident, nor overly eager, as he rolled up his shirt sleeves.

Quantrelle moved in with both fists cocked and his tall body tipped over. "Never mind the sleeves," he warned, and pitched forward so abruptly that Barton barely dodged the first swing at his face.

It was an odd thing. Instead of countering, Barton covered up, taking a barrage of blows on his guarding arms. Quantrelle loosed a hoot of jeering laughter. This was just what he'd suspected: *Hal Barton was yellow!*

He got through the big man's guard for a glancing right jab to the face, then slugged him hard in the belly. Barton back-tracked, colliding with Jeddy's horse. Jeddy stuck a boot in his back and pushed him toward Quantrelle who came charging in. "Fight, damn you — fight!" Quantrelle ordered.

That rash command seemed to anger Barton. He lunged into a two-fisted attack that caught Quantrelle unprepared — that knocked him off balance so that he went to one knee.

"Pour it on him!" Shambrun urged in his high, cackling voice.

Barton kicked at Quantrelle's face, missing it as Quantrelle got up taking the boot against his left shoulder.

"Real mean, aren't you?" Quantrelle jeered, understanding now that Barton's strategy was to play a waiting game — to lure him into carelessness. Two could play that game, but Quantrelle thought: *To hell with it!* Charging in he grazed Barton's face with a right, turned as the Pool boss turned and caught him in the kidneys with a chopping left.

Barton loosed a gusty curse, tried to whirl clear and cursed again as Quantrelle targeted his nose with a solid smash to the face. That blow seemed to confuse Barton; his right hand came up, its palm shielding his nose, and in this moment he was as wide open as a man could be. Quantrelle drove a right to Barton's belly that doubled him over, then slugged him in the face with both fists. As from a far distance he heard Jim Jeddy exclaim, "Somebody comin' up the road — looks like Chalice."

171

But a flare of pure savagery was in Quantrelle now, and the words held no meaning. Here in front of him was the sadistic son who'd pounded a held man without mercy. He slammed a blood-smeared fist into Barton's face, and when Barton started to go down, grasped him by the shirt front and propped him up.

"Now you're the held man," Quantrelle said pantingly, and slugged him in the jaw.

Barton's knees buckled instantly. His whole body went limp, the weight of it so dead that Quantrelle couldn't hold him up with one hand. He slapped Barton's down-tilted face as the Pool boss fell and said disgustedly, "You gutless counterfeit."

He was standing there above Barton's sprawled form, wiping bloody knuckles on a pants leg, when Jim Chalice rode up and demanded, "What's going on here?"

Quantrelle grinned, "Just repaying a social obligation, is all," he said and walked over to his horse in the relaxed fashion of a thoroughly contented man.

Jeddy still held his gun. He waited until Quantrelle was in saddle, then said to Chalice, "I wouldn't let nobody borry that pistol if I was you."

And he rode half-turned in saddle, warily watching, as he followed Quantrelle out of

172

the yard.

Presently, as they came to the stage road, Quantrelle halted, canting his head to listen. There was no sound of pursuit. He glanced at his bruised knuckles and grinned and said cheerfully, "That deal worked out nice, Jim — real nice."

Jeddy shrugged. "You could of shot Barton a lot easier," he muttered. "That's how it'll be in the long run, anyway. Either you shoot him, or he shoots you."

"Shouldn't wonder," Quantrelle agreed. "But I owed him that whipping, regardless."

There was in Quantrelle now a fine sense of accomplishment. A man didn't often have the satisfaction of ramrodding a marriage and mauling a rascal the same day. It called for some sort of celebration. So thinking, Quantrelle brought out the loose change in his pocket; counting it, he said, "Enough for a couple drinks apiece, Jim. Let's ride to town."

Jeddy smiled, said, "Good idea, friend. I ain't bellied up to the Belvedere bar in nigh onto a month."

"We'll drink a toast to the bride and groom," Quantrelle suggested, and now, as two riders came around a bend in the road, he asked, "Pool members?"

Jeddy nodded. "The young one is Bill

Peeble, the other is Gus Anderson. They've got homesteads on Squawk Creek."

Quantrelle eyed the oncoming pair, observing their shabby clothing and make-shift saddle gear. The poverty of hardscrabble homesteads was etched into their gaunt, whisker-bristled faces; it was a harassment in their eyes. Watching them come up in the slow, wary way of men unsure of their reception Quantrelle thought: *They'll lose what little they have to Hal Barton in the end,* and felt a nagging sense of pity.

Peeble, who looked to be in his middle twenties, said, "Howdy, Jim."

Jeddy nodded, not speaking as they passed.

"Do those men have families?" Quantrelle inquired.

"Yeah, Peeble has two kids and Gus has five or six."

Quantrelle thought about that as they rode on toward Tailholt. He said, "It doesn't seem fitting to fight men who've got families to feed. What happens to those kids if their fathers get killed?"

Jeddy shrugged. "That's their worry, not ours, friend Clay. Let them that has the woman fun have the worry that goes with it. A man who sleeps by hisself shouldn't fret about what happens to somebody else's kids."

It was, Quantrelle reflected, a realistic and comfortable philosophy. There was no use worrying about what couldn't be helped. He grinned at Jim, saying, "A year from now Red will have a young one to worry about feeding."

When they rode into town Quantrelle called a friendly greeting to Joe Pardee who sat on his bench in the stable doorway. He said to Jeddy, "In case you don't know it, there's a friend of Apache Pat." And recalling how the liveryman had warned him of a probable ambush, added, "A good friend of mine, also."

The Swenson team and buckboard stood at the hotel hitchrack; recognizing it, Jeddy said, "They must be havin' a weddin' supper in the dinin' room. Wish old Red would come out and give us a invite. I could use a bait of grub myself."

It was coming sundown now and Quantrelle mused, "It's eating time, but we can't eat and drink both, Jim. Which will it be?"

"Drink," Jeddy said without hesitation.

Quantrelle grinned, feeling a kindred need, and a queerly urgent anticipation. Instead of drinking to offset the jitters of a shootout he'd drink to celebrate a satisfying accomplishment. Two of them in fact. Dismounting at the Belvedere tie-rail he said, "A drink for each one," and accompanied Jeddy into the saloon.

There were three customers at the bar, one a glassware drummer exhibiting a sample case of merchandise to the fat-faced bartender, and the other two teamsters, by the look of them. Quantrelle saw a frown rut the saloonman's heavy-jowled face as he identified his new customers. Remembering how this fat booze dispenser had spoiled his chance for a fast getaway night before last, Quantrelle thought: *Another one that needs slapping down.*

"Come on Jud, we're thirsty," Jim urged, and as the saloonman came toward them, ordered, "Bourbon."

"Me too," Quantrelle said.

When Jud brought bottle and glasses, Quantrelle asked, "Is this one on the house?"

Jud stared at him, asked, "Why should it be?"

"Well, you owe me a drink. Several drinks in fact."

"What for?" Jud demanded.

"For sicking the dogs on me night before last," Quantrelle explained, and drawing his gun, laid it on the bar. "Isn't that correct?"

Jud glanced at the gun. Then he peered at Quantrelle in bug-eyed astonishment. "You threatenin' me?" he asked.

"No friend, I'm giving you a chance to do the right thing," Quantrelle said. "Is this one on the house?"

Jud nodded, and plodded back to the glassware drummer, whereupon Quantrelle grinned and announced: "Have a drink, men — it's on the house."

The two teamsters brought their glasses which Quantrelle filled to overflowing, along with Jeddy's and his own. Then he asked, "What's the apron's full name, Jim?"

"Jud Pendergast," Jeddy said, and one of the teamsters corrected this, saying, "Judson G. Pendergast, accordin' to the sign outside."

Quantrelle raised his brimming glass. "To Judson C. Pendergast who pays his obligations like a gentleman should!" he toasted.

The bourbon warmed his empty stomach. It increased the pleasant glow of satisfaction and prompted an urgent wish to share it with the others. Turning to Jeddy, he said, "Go get Pardee."

"Sure," Jim agreed, and hurried to the batwings.

Quantrelle heard him shout an invitation to the liveryman from the stoop; he watched

Pendergast, enjoying the bartender's pained expression. "We need another glass," Quantrelle ordered.

Now Jim Jeddy came to the batwings and said, "The Swensons just drove away from the hotel. How about us askin' Red over for a drink?"

"By all means," Quantrelle agreed, and waggling a finger at Pendergast, announced, "Make it two glasses, Jud."

It was a matter of moments then until Red and Pardee had increased the lineup to six, whereupon Quantrelle filled the glasses and called to Pendergast, "Is this on the house also, Jud?"

The saloonman shrugged, glanced at Quantrelle's gun, and nodded.

"A toast to Tailholt's newest husband — Red Parmalee, the most fortunate of men!"

It seemed no more than reasonble that there should be a toast for the bride, and now Red demanded that Pendergast and the drummer join the happy throng. "Everybody has to drink to Fern — the prettiest goddam wife in Rincon Basin!"

The drummer quickly accepted his invitation, and when Red reached for Quantrelle's gun, Jud Pendergast said sourly, "All right — all right."

Oddly enough it was Jim Jeddy who suggested kissing the bride. "This is a weddin' celebration, ain't it?" he demanded. "Its only fittin' we should kiss the blushin' bride!"

Quantrelle saw at once that Red didn't like that idea. The redhead muttered something about "staggy old goats," and now, as the glassware drummer took up the suggestion, Parmalee said, "No, by God! The man that kisses my wife will have to lick me first!"

Which was when Fern called from the batwings, "Red — I'm waiting for you, honey."

Embarrassment painted Parmalee's freckled face a blazing red; he called, "I'm comin' right now," and hurried to his waiting wife.

Jim Jeddy was disgusted. "What good is a weddin' celebration if you don't git to kiss the bride?" he complained drunkenly.

He was still voicing his opinions on that score when he rode from town with Quantrelle fifteen minutes later. "Red is downright stingy," he insisted. "Look at all the fun he'll have — and us not one measly little kiss."

Quantrelle laughed, hugely enjoying the whole deal. "We had us a celebration," he mused contentedly. "We did for a fact."

■ ■ ■ ■

Oley Swenson was unhitching his team by lantern light when Mike Halloran rode up to the corral and asked, "Why wasn't you to the meetin', Oley?"

"Because I had more important business in town," Swenson said cheerfully. "My girl got married this afternoon, Mike. I put on a wedding supper with all the fixin's at the hotel."

Halloran, who'd lived alone on his ranch in Sabino Canyon since his wife had died a year ago, exclaimed, "Why that's fine, Oley! Who'd Fern marry?"

"Red Parmalee," Swenson said, adding defensively, "I tried to break it up, Mike — not likin' the idee at first. But you can't stop romantic notions in the young. Red is a trifle on the wild side, but he'll settle down, now that he's got a married man's obligations."

"Shouldn't wonder," Halloran agreed. "But 'tis a queer mixup, Oley — you bein' a member of the Pool, and Red a Big T rider. A real queer mixup, bejasus."

Swenson nodded agreement. "That's the part I didn't like," he admitted. "But there was nothin' I could do about it. Fern had

180

her heart set on Red. She thinks he's the only man in the world that's worth his salt."

"Everybody to their own opinions," Halloran mused, expressing none of his own in regard to Red Parmalee. Then he said, "The Pool is goin' into action tomorrow, Oley. It was decided that we'd meet at Barton's place, bringin' blankets and extry horses."

"What for?" Swenson asked.

"To bust up Big T's roundup. Hal figgers they'll start gatherin' beef tomorrow. Accordin' to Ike Gallatin the roundup will start in the Kettle Drum Hills. At least that was how it was planned. We're to meet at nine o'clock, so's to get up there about noon."

Swenson turned the team into the corral. He asked, "Did Jim Chalice agree to this roundup raid?"

"That he did," Halloran reported, "although 'twas plain he had no real likin' for it. But after the way them Big T bums pulled down his garden fence the other night, Jim ain't quite so peaceable minded. He agrees with Barton now that it's a fight — or be drove off our places, one at a time."

"But raidin' a roundup is downright Injun," Oley protested. "It ain't as if Big T was goin to shove them cattle onto our grass, or crowd us in any way. Them steers is headed for market."

181

"For one purpose," Halloran pointed out. "To git cash money for bullets to shoot at us, and pay gun wages to them that use 'em." Then he asked abruptly, "It wouldn't be in your mind to quit the Pool, would it, Oley?"

Swenson shook his head. "But I'm not raidin' no roundup," he said flatly. "Leastwise not till Big T raids one of mine."

Halloran thought about that for a moment. Finally he said, " 'Tis your privilege to do as you see fit, Oley," and rode on out of the yard.

Clay Quantrelle was pulling off his boots in the bunkhouse when Sonora came in and said, "Senor Swenson ees up on the ridge. Says thees of the importance to see you, *muy pronto.*"

"So?" Quantrelle mused, glancing at Jim Jeddy who was asleep in a lower bunk, with Kid Calhoun snoring loudly in the bunk above him. Gramp Pettigrue had grudgingly warmed up a late supper, after which Quantrelle had spent a brief interval of final planning with Apache Pat.

Tugging a boot back on, Quantrelle said, "You might as well turn in, Sonora. I'll root the Kid out for his late watch."

"Gracias," Sonora agreed, grinning his

happiness. "She weel be *mucho trabajo manana.*"

"Much work tomorrow is right," Quantrelle agreed.

Borrowing the Mexican's horse he rode past the dark house and up the winding, slotted trail. What, he wondered, would be important enough to bring Swenson out at this time of night? It must be prompted by more than a desire to express appreciation for arranging Fern's marriage . . .

Oley greeted him on the rim, asking, "That you, Quantrelle?"

"Yeah," Quantrelle said. "What's up?"

Swenson drew in close, then spoke in a confidential tone that was little above a whisper, "I've got it on good authority that Barton's bunch will hit your roundup about noon tomorrow. They plan to jump you in the Kettle Drums."

That news surprised Quantrelle. How, he wondered, did the Pool know exactly where the gather would begin? Then he thought of Gallatin and cursed softly. That was it, of course. Ike knew Apache Pat's plans — and understood the urgent necessity for gathering the beef in the shortest possible time. Knowing Big T range as he did, Gallatin could call the turn exactly; would know where each circle was likely to be made and the most likely location for each night's camp.

"Much obliged for the tip," Quantrelle said.

"Figgered I owed it to you," Oley muttered. "It goes agin the grain to turn informer. Never thought I'd do such a thing. But you done me a big favor — just about the biggest favor a man could do. And it didn't seem fittin' for me not to warn you."

Guessing how hard a chore it had been, Quantrelle felt sorry for Swenson. The man was torn between two sets of loyalties now . . .

"You going to be in on the raid?" Quantrelle asked.

"No, by grab. I told Barton it was too Injun for me, and I told Mike Halloran the same thing when he stopped by my place tonight. I ain't got no love for Tanner but I didn't cotton to this deal, even before Red married Fern. Now it seems loco for me to be shootin' at my son-in-law, or at the man who talked him into marryin' my girl." Then he said, "It has me tol'able puzzled how you done it, mister."

Quantrelle chuckled. "Just a case of fatherly advice," he explained. "Red jumped at it, once he saw how right it was — and all."

"And I was figgerin' to gun him," Oley said. "It would of been awful if I did — purely awful."

"Which is how the raid will be tomorrow," Quantrelle muttered morosely. "Even knowing about it, we can't stop it — and we can't be looking over our shoulders while we're working cattle. We'll just have to go on about our business until the first shot is fired. After that it'll be dog-eat-dog and there'll be more than one empty saddle before it's finished."

Knowing that one of those empty saddles might belong to Jim Chalice, he added urgently, "I sure wish there was some way to head it off — any way at all."

For a long moment of silence they both thought about it, then Swenson said, "If we had a sheriff that had any guts there might be a way. But not with George Weaver."

"What could a sheriff do?" Quantrelle asked, seeing no solution in that direction.

"Well, he could arrest Ike Gallatin for shootin' Tanner," Swenson explained.

"Only on suspicion," Quantrelle muttered. "Nobody saw Ike do it."

"That makes it all the better, then. The sheriff could also arrest Hal Barton and that new man he's got workin' for him — all on suspicion. But Weaver wouldn't try such a

185

hazardous chore. He'd rather sit and guzzle booze than do his duty."

Quantrelle nodded agreement. George, he thought, could hardly be expected to handle a deal like that. And even if he did, with proper help, it wouldn't amount to anything. Other Pool members, enraged at so raw a maneuver, would express their resentment by going through with the raid anyway. And some of them would be shot down, along with Big T riders, in the process.

But now a different angle came to Quantrelle — a startling possibility that caused him to exclaim, "By God, I think you've hit on something, Oley! You're in the right church — but the wrong pew!"

"What you mean by that?" Swenson demanded.

"Instead of arresting Gallatin, Barton and Shambrun why not arrest the other Pool members — the ones we don't want hurt?"

"But what could you arrest them for?" Swenson asked. "They ain't done nothin'."

Quantrelle chuckled, sure now that he was right. "George Weaver came up with the right answer night before last. He said the only way Pool members could be kept from committing suicide was to handcuff them. Well, that's what we'll do — arrest Chalice, Halloran, Peeble and Anderson. We'll keep them in jail until the beef gather is finished, so there'll be no raid."

"But you got no charge against 'em," Swenson protested.

"Sure we have — a damn good charge."

"What?"

"Suspicion of shooting Pat Tanner," Quantrelle announced. "Somebody shot him. Nobody saw the man who did it, so we suspect them all."

Swenson thought about that for a long moment. Finally he said, "It might work, if Weaver was a real sheriff. But he ain't got the guts to put it over. He won't even try."

"He will when I get through with him," Quantrelle promised. "He'll try like he never tried before."

Swenson didn't question that confident announcement. Instead he said, "I thought you was loco in your head when you told me Red would marry Fern within three days. If you say Weaver will tackle this thing I'm willin' to reckon he will."

"With proper help," Quantrelle explained, "George will have four high class deputies working with him."

"You, Jeddy, Sonora and Kid Calhoun," Swenson mused. "I guess it'll be too early in the morning for Red to git in on it."

"Yeah," Quantrelle agreed. "Red will be

out of the play and so will you. Don't leave your dooryard tomorrow, Oley. And if Hal Barton stops by, act like you haven't seen or heard a thing."

Then he rode back down the trail, knowing how reluctant George Weaver would be, and thinking: *This one time he's going to do his duty if I have to pistol-whip him.*

It wasn't quite that difficult. Awakened from sound sleep in the middle of the night, Weaver briefly balked at the idea, insisting it wasn't legal . . .

"I've got no right to arrest all them men, even to keep 'em from bein' killed," he protested. "Everybody knows Jim Chalice wouldn't try to murder a man in cold blood. Neither would Bill Peeble or none of the others you want arrested. It'd look downright scandalous."

"Perhaps so," Quantrelle admitted quietly. "But you're going to do it, George. You're going to swear us in as deputies and do your share of the arresting."

"Suppose I don't?" Weaver asked half-heartedly.

Quantrelle sighed. "There's no question about whether you'll do it or not, George. The only question is how you look when we start out."

Then Quantrelle held up his right hand

so that lamplight shone on the bruised knuckles. "A sheriff with two black eyes and a busted nose would look downright comical riding into town today," he mused.

Weaver, looking short and frail standing there in his bare feet and dangling suspenders, said resignedly, "I'm too old a man to fight a young buck like you."

And presently, when Quantrelle had awakened the others and Gramp Pettigrue grumpily called them to breakfast, George muttered, "I knowed he was a heller, first time I ever seen him, by God."

CHAPTER SIX

Jim Chalice saddled up at his corral before sunrise while Eve watched, wearing a red shawl against the morning's chill. "I should be home by suppertime," he predicted, and as he rode from the yard, called back, "Don't worry if I'm late."

Eve, he reflected, would be worried aplenty if she knew what the plans were for today. He was worried himself. Turning in saddle to wave farewell, he wondered if he would ride into his dooryard again at sundown — or be carried in.

Chalice frowned, dreading the ordeal ahead of him. Even though Hal Barton's reasoning was right, it seemed like an awful thing to do. For this wouldn't be a spasmodic, spur-of-the-moment fight; it would be a deliberate attack, calmly planned ahead of time.

That was the part that stuck in Jim Chalice's craw — that formed a cold knot of revulsion in his stomach. But a man couldn't just sit with folded hands when his home was threatened. No matter how peaceable he was, he couldn't avoid the trouble that cursed this range like a blight. Those Big T fence-busters had proved that. It was fight now, as Hal said, or be forced out of Rincon Basin by Tanner's hard-case crew.

"A sorry choice," Chalice muttered, and now noticed fresh hoofprints in the road's deep dust. Four or five horses, he reckoned, studying the tracks; and wondered why that many riders had headed toward town this early. Yet even so, Chalice was taken completely by surprise when Sheriff George Weaver rode from the brush with a leveled gun in his hand.

"You're under arrest," Weaver announced.

Chalice stared at the gun in bug-eyed astonishment. "Arrest!" he echoed disbelievingly. "What for?"

"On suspicion of shooting Pat Tanner."

Chalice peered at Weaver as if eyeing a lunatic. "You must be out of your head," he scoffed. "What kind of a frame-up is this anyway?"

Weaver shrugged, his watery eyes not meeting Chalice's gaze directly. He said, "I know it looks a trifle odd, Jim. But I'm takin' you to jail. That's final."

Ten miles northeast at almost this same moment . . .

Bill Peeble was eating breakfast with his wife and two tow-headed youngsters when Jim Jeddy appeared at the kitchen doorway with a gun in his hand. Mrs. Peeble screamed, and her astonished husband asked shakily, "What you doin' here at this time of day?"

"I'm arrestin' you on suspicion," Jeddy announced. "Saddle up and we'll go to town."

"What right you got to arrest anybody?" Peeble demanded.

"George Weaver made me a deputy sheriff," the Big T rider said meekly. But there was no meekness in his unblinking eyes, nor in the way he held the gun. "Come on, Bill. I'm in somewhat of a hurry. We're startin' our beef gather today."

"What if I say no?" Peeble asked, outraged at the thought of surrendering in front of his two boys who considered their father a fearless devil of a man.

"You'll come with me, alive or otherwise," Jeddy said flatly.

"Please go with him, Bill!" Mrs. Peeble pleaded nervously. "Can't you see he's just itchin' to pull that trigger?"

A mirthless smile edged Jeddy's thin lips. "You got sharp eyes, ma'am," he praised, and stepping swiftly around Peeble, prodded him out of the house.

They were crossing through pine timber west of Gus Anderson's place when Kid Calhoun cut into the trail . . .

"Wasn't Gus at home?" Jeddy asked.

The Kid nodded, and explained sheepishly, "Gus wouldn't believe I was a deputy on account of me not havin' a badge, or nothin' to prove it. He just figgered I was funnin'."

"Why didn't you show him different?" Jeddy demanded.

Kid Calhoun shrugged. "Well, I couldn't shoot him, Jim — not in front of his wife and them five kids. All I could do was try to spook him into comin' with me, and he don't spook worth a dam."

Jim grunted disgustedly. "I thought you was tough," he jibed, "listenin' to all the bunkhouse brags you been makin'. Well, we got to bring him in, one way or another."

Turning to Peeble he ordered, "Ride over to Anderson's in front of us, Bill. Gus won't shoot you — but I will, if you try any tricks."

■ ■ ■ ■

At the Arrow H in Sabino Canyon . . .

Tousel-haired, shirtless and with his suspenders dangling, old Mike Halloran stepped from his bachelor shack with a bucket in his hand shortly before sunrise. He was at the pump, propelling its squeaky handle, when a man he'd never seen before rode into the yard and announced, "You're under arrest."

"Who be you?" Halloran demanded.

"Name of Quantrelle," the tall stranger said. "I'm George Weaver's deputy."

Old Mike peered up at Quantrelle's bruised face. "Ye look like a bar room bum to me," he muttered crankily. "Where's yer badge?"

"Right here," Quantrelle replied. He took the star from his pocket and pinned it on his vest. It was the only extra badge that Weaver had.

"Then where's yer warrant?"

"Haven't got one," Quantrelle admitted.

"Then how the hell can ye arrest anybody?"

Quantrelle smiled, and waggled his gun. "With this," he said. "Put on your shirt and come along."

"And what if I don't choose to come?" Halloran asked.

Ignoring the question, Quantrelle said quietly, "You're coming," and something in his eyes caused the old Irishman to exclaim, "I believe yer right, Bucko. I believe you be!"

Some ten or twelve miles to the southwest, Sonora sat his horse in a jumble of huge boulders on a low ridge that overlooked Barton's place. A thin blue spiral of smoke rose string straight from the chimney and for a time Sonora waited in the patient fashion of a man long accustomed to waiting. Cradling his Winchester against his belly he shaped a cigarette and had it half smoked when Barton came out of the cabin doorway.

"Bueno," Sonora murmured, lifting his rifle and taking careful aim.

He fired, observing the spurt of dust his bullet kicked up a few feet in front of Barton and a trifle to the left. The Pool boss halted instantly, peering about as if uncertain where the slug had come from; then, as Sonora fired again, Barton whirled in swift retreat.

A remote tinkle of breaking glass drifted up to Sonora, telling him that Barton was getting set to return the fire. The Big T rider grinned, knowing that the distance was too great for accurate shooting. And remembering that his instructions were to keep out of range. "Just hold those three inside the cabin for a couple hours," Quantrelle had said. "And don't get yourself shot. We're short handed for the roundup."

There was a burst of shooting from the cabin; three guns by the sound of it. But none of those bullets came very close to Sonora. He didn't fire again until a man showed himself in the doorway. Allowing for the distance, Sonora aimed high, and chuckled as the door slammed shut.

Keeping a wary watch behind him, in case this shooting attracted some Pool member not taken in by the posse, Sonora saw a plume of dust boil up above the brush out toward the stage road. Firing a final shot at the cabin he backed his horse out of the boulders and was waiting beside the road when Red Parmalee drove up with his bride sharing the seat of a livery rig.

"What's goin' on?" Red demanded.

Sonora shrugged. "A leetle game of loco, I am theenking. Senor Quantrelle orders that you stay at the ranch ontil thees game of loco ees done."

"Where is Quantrelle?" Parmalee asked, wholly puzzled.

"Quien sabe?" Sonora shrugged. "He ees now the deputy of law and the crew she rides all night."

Then, glancing at Fern who sat close to her husband, Sonora said slyly, "Much better for you, Red — weeth the woman and a bed in town. Thees deputy of the law life ees no good."

Wild rumor and report ran the length and breadth of Tailholt. Sheriff Weaver, according to gossip, had gone completely berserk, deputizing the entire Big T crew and arresting all members of the Pool. Or killing them. One story had it that Hal Barton was dead — shot down resisting arrest.

"Tanner's gunslingers have took over the whole range," a townsman reported. "That's why he imported that Lincoln County killer!"

By noon four of the Pool's members were in the big cell at the rear of the jail and Quantrelle was giving his final instructions to Jim Jeddy . . .

"You and the Kid pick up Sonora on your way to the ranch. Start out with the wagon this afternoon so the gather can begin first thing in the morning. I'll join you soon as I get things settled here."

Jeddy nodded, and turning toward the

hitchrack, predicted ominously, "This deal may take some settlin', friend Clay — more settlin' than you Figger on."

"Perhaps," Quantrelle admitted. Watching Jim and Kid Calhoun ride off, he wondered how soon the showdown would come.

Not until tonight, he thought, and going into Weaver's office, glanced speculatively at the sheriff. Weaver was nervous as a cat. He'd had nothing to drink since leaving Big T and the strain was telling on his booze-jangled nerves.

Now he said, "Guess I'll go git somethin' to eat."

"Be sure it's something to *eat*," Quantrelle counselled. "I want you sober, George — stark, church deacon sober."

Then, in a more friendly tone, he added, "You're not siding Apache Pat now. This is bigger than that — the biggest thing you've ever done. You're helping to save honest Pool members from committing suicide."

Weaver nodded. He started to go, then turned and asked, "Would it be all right for me to tell Mae why we put them four in jail — if she promises not to tell it?"

"Sure," Quantrelle said, and saw a bright hopefulness come into Weaver's bloodshot eyes. George, he supposed, wanted to square himself with Mae Bowen; wanted to impress her with the fact that for once he was doing a brave and unselfish thing.

I'd like to do the same thing with Eve, Quantrelle thought a trifle enviously. And knew there'd be no chance of convincing her.

Afterwards, sitting at the boot-scarred desk, Quantrelle listened to the drone of conversation that drifted down the jail hallway. Bill Peeble seemed to be doing most of the talking, but presently Quantrelle heard Jim Chalice say wrathfully, "It's not George Weaver's fault. He was forced into doing what he did. You can't blame George for being afraid of Quantrelle. The man is a cold-blooded killer."

And Mike Halloran said gustily, "That he is, begorrah. I could see it in his eyes. There's a spalpeen look to him that chills yer blood."

Quantrelle smiled thinly. None of those yonder men would believe him if he told the real reason they'd been jailed. Chalice and his friends would never understand why they were here. Nor would Eve. That was the part of it that would turn this deal into a hollow victory no matter how successfully it turned out. At the end he would be accused of smashing the Rincon Basin Pool; would stand charged with Hal Barton's death. For there was no doubt in Quantrelle's mind about one thing; sooner or later it would be as Jim Jeddy had predicted — "Either you shoot him, or he shoots you."

Sheriff Weaver returned with a huge tray piled high with food. "Got to treat our prisoners right," he announced, and there was a prideful glint in his eyes when he added, "Mae thinks I'm doin' a big thing. She acted downright proud of me, by God!"

Quantrelle grinned, sincerely pleased to hear that George was in good standing with his woman again. A man could go without sleep, or food, or water for a long time and still keep going if there was a woman waiting for him when the work was done. It gave him something to look forward to; something to warm his blood and put an itch of eagerness in him, no matter how tired or hungry he was. It made that much difference . . .

A cool breeze slanted across the garden where Eve Chalice dug up what was left of her summer carrot crop. There was a hint of approaching winter in the air this afternoon, even though the sun shone intermittently through high-banked clouds, it gave little warmth.

Eve worked slowly, wanting the chore to

last. This need for working in the soil — for planting and tending a vegetable garden — had been born in her, she supposed. It was the one thing her mother had liked about ranch life. The only thing.

Eve smiled, remembering how a confused teen-aged girl had been puzzled by a mother who seemed to adore and despise her husband at the same time. An actress accustomed to town living, her mother had been both loyal and rebellious. Bob had inherited some of his mother's rebel ways, and now Eve thought: *It must be a family trait.* For she had accepted kisses from a man who worked for her father's sworn enemy. A man whose bullet might one day kill the best father a girl ever had . . .

Toting the last gunnysack of carrots to the house, Eve wondered if Clay Quantrelle knew about the Pool meeting yesterday and what it signified. Her father hadn't said much about it, but he seemed resigned to the fact there'd be a pitched battle against Big T before it was over. The grim way he'd cleaned and oiled his Winchester last night had convinced Eve that a raid was pending. The portent of it had plagued her with a sense of foreboding when she watched him ride off this morning. It still nagged her.

Eve frowned, and tried to shake off the

dismal sense of apprehension. She recalled how Clay Quantrelle had said there'd be no peace while Hal Barton lived. That didn't make sense, unless Clay meant that Hal would never bow to Pat Tanner's domination of the range . . .

Recalling all that had happened last night, Eve wondered what Clay had been on the point of telling her. And why he'd changed his mind. She had thought about it, lying awake long after Clay had ridden off. He didn't seem to be a secretive man, nor one who'd hesitate to say what he thought. And there was nothing bashful about him. She'd known that the first time they met — had read it in the bold appraisal of his eyes. And he had proved it again last night. Remembering how possessively he had taken her into his arms, Eve smiled. It wasn't fitting, she supposed, to admit even to herself that she liked to remember how he had kissed her. But she did, and feeling the hotness come into her cheeks, understood that just the memory of Clay Quantrelle's embrace could make her blush.

Again, as she had last night, Eve endeavored to convince herself that he was just a brazen drifter, well versed in handling women. *He probably laughed at me afterward,* she thought. For despite his passionate actions she had detected what seemed to be a faintly concealed contempt in him, as if he suspected all women were easy.

She was considering that, and resenting its implications, when she saw Jim Jeddy, Sonora and Kid Calhoun ride past the front gate. They were traveling at an easy lope, and seemed in no particular hurry — more like men returning from a successful assignment. Eve watched them go on toward the Big T fork, and thought: *Perhaps there's been a fight at Hal's place!*

And hard on the heels of that came the throat-clutching premonition that something had happened to her father . . .

"I'll go see," she said abruptly. "I'll go right now."

Clay Quantrelle went to the Empire for a late noon meal, choosing a table near a front window where he could watch the plaza. This was around three o'clock and the diningroom was deserted. Mae Bowen took his order, remaining long enough to say, "Even if I can't believe what George says about Hal Barton, I'm proud of him just the same."

"You should be," Quantrelle said pleasantly. "George is a fine man, when you get to know him."

Mae laughed derisively, saying, "I know George Weaver, inside and out and there's nothing fine about him. There used to be, before he started guzzling whiskey and taking his orders from Pat Tanner. But not now."

"But I thought you said you were proud of him," Quantrelle said, wholly puzzled.

"I'm proud to learn that he hasn't sunk so low but what he's able to do an unselfish thing," Mae explained. "But from what I hear you scared him into it."

Quantrelle shrugged, and watching her go to the kitchen, decided there was no use attempting to understand what went on in a woman's mind. Easing back in the chair he sighed wearily, more tired, somehow, than the lack of one night's sleep should make him. *Must be getting old,* he thought, and kept watch on the plaza. Hal Barton might decide to hurry this deal up a trifle — might make a try at the jail before dark.

"No telling what that twisty son will do," Quantrelle mused.

The thought came to him that he had been watching for Barton the first time he ate in this diningroom — as he was now. It seemed like a long time ago, so much had happened since that day. He hadn't kissed Eve Chalice then, nor known she was engaged to a sadistic scoundrel who wanted to be king of Rincon Basin. All he'd known was that Eve was the most desirable woman he'd ever met.

Thinking about her now he wondered what she would think when her father failed to return home this evening . . .

Mae brought his meal, not speaking as she served him. He picked up the cup of coffee, said, "Please bring me another," and proceeded to drink it before eating.

Quantrelle was sampling his second cup of coffee when he saw Scarface Shambrun cross the plaza with a small bundle in his hands. He thought instantly: *Barton must be in town,* and got up from the table.

As he left the diningroom Mae Bowen called, "You coming back?"

"Perhaps," Quantrelle said; reaching the veranda and seeing Shambrun join Hal Barton and Ike Gallatin in front of the sheriff's office, he thought: *Perhaps not.*

Hal Barton's bull-toned voice came across the plaza, ordering, "Open up, George — or we'll blast you out with dynamite!"

People were gathering from all directions; excited, curious people anticipating a spectacular event. Quantrelle cursed himself for not having opened the window near his table so that he could listen as well as watch.

He hadn't heard any of this commotion — hadn't even suspected that Barton was in town until he glimpsed Shambrun. And now, knowing that the bundle contained several sticks of dynamite, Quantrelle understood that he had lost. George Weaver wouldn't hold out against such a threat . . .

So thinking, Quantrelle went down the steps, nudging his gun loose in its leather — wondering how near the jail he would get before those three became aware of him. It wasn't possible that he could approach close enough to get the drop on them. Yet even as that realization raced through his mind, Quantrelle thought: *Everyone is watching the jail. They may not notice me!*

It was a thin, flimsy fragment of hope. A fragile straw to cling to as he tromped across the plaza's powdery dust. Across the hoof-pocked, sunlit dust that muffled the sound of his boots. He was a quarter of the way across now, passing gawk-eyed townsmen whose attention was strictly focused on the sheriff's office.

I'm going to make it! Quantrelle thought, the fingers of his right hand hovering close to holster. A swift-rising sense of anticipation ran through him so that he was no longer pessimistic, nor tired. Another few steps and he would be close enough to get the drop on those three who were angrily arguing with George Weaver.

Then, as he had once before, Jud Pendergast loosed a warning from the Belvedere stoop: "Quantrelle!" he shouted. "Behind you, Hal!"

A sighing curse slipped from Quantrelle's lips. In this frantic moment of drawing his gun and firing it he knew that he was doomed; knew there'd be no surviving those three guns. For even though Ike Gallatin's left arm was in a sling, the ex-ramrod had a gun in his good right hand.

Quantrelle fired as those three whirled. He saw Gallatin jerk sideways, as if hit, and felt an obscure astonishment that his first shot had missed Barton by that wide a margin. For there was in him an unrelenting decision to live long enough to kill Hal Barton, and so his aim had been at the Pool boss.

He fired again, and now, as a woman screamed somewhere off to the left, Quantrelle felt Barton's bullet slice hide from the upper muscle of his right arm. Quantrelle dropped to one knee and took time for deliberate aim at Barton's blocky, dust-hazed shape. Another bullet whined wickedly past his head, so close he felt the wind lash of its passing. But it didn't spoil the accuracy of his aim, nor keep him from slamming two additional slugs into Barton's crazily floundering body.

Shambrun, who had taken time to put down the dynamite and rush swiftly away from it, was firing now from behind a gnarled mesquite tree at the north edge of the plaza. Quantrelle shot at him, saw bark fly from the tree and knew he had missed; knew also that there was only one bullet left in his gun. This fight, he thought, would be soon over. There'd be no time to reload. But even as he thumbed back the hammer for his final shot, a gun blasted across the plaza and Shambrun staggered away from the tree. The yonder gun exploded again while Shambrun tipped over, its slug knocking him flat on his face.

A sudden hush, hugely exaggerated in the wake of barking guns, settled on the plaza. Quantrelle turned to stare at the sheriff's office — at the most unexpected sight he had ever seen. For George Weaver stood in the doorway with a smoking gun in his hand. *And George was proudly smiling!*

Quantrelle loosed a gusty sigh and understood now why Gallatin had gone down. It hadn't been his bullet that hit Ike; George Weaver had targeted him with his first shot. And with that astounding knowledge rifling through him, Quantrelle understood why a Lincoln County renegade had survived again today. The difference between life and death here had been made up of queer ingredients, he reflected. A boozy lawman's dream of romance had been part of it. There'd been George Weaver's need to be a man at long last, the stiff, unbending pride of a middle-aged waitress — and a lot of luck.

Idly, as if he were a disinterested spectator, Quantrelle watched Mae Bowen hurry across the plaza, pushing people out of her way as she ran toward Sheriff Weaver . . .

"George!" she called to him, and now, as he came to meet her, Mae cried, "I'm proud of you, George — proud!"

Joe Pardee tromped up to Quantrelle, a fresh chaw of tobacco bulging his left cheek so that he looked like a grinning squirrel. "Your scheme worked out perfect," he praised. "But you was lucky, by God — awful lucky!"

Clay Quantrelle didn't feel lucky. He felt old and lonely and morose. For it had been a hollow victory, as he'd known it would be. If either Gallatin or Shambrun had survived there might have been a chance of forcing a confession of Barton's fantastic plan. But they were both dead.

The folks in Tailholt would refuse to believe George Weaver's story. They'd figure that the jailing of the Pool members had been a crafty ruse to draw Barton into a slaughter trap. And that wasn't long in coming, for with the sounds of the gun battle dying away, they began to stick their noses out. It wasn't long before a crowd had gathered. Practically everybody had come, even the womenfolk from the outlying ranches.

The muttering was general and even Joe Pardee had spoken up angrily. "A scheme to bust the Pool, once and for all."

Clay said nothing, hoping the crowd would disperse but it didn't turn out that way. If anything, it got worse and a streak of hardness developed as several of the townspeople condemned in loud voices the brutal gun battle and the maneuvering which led up to it.

Even then, trouble might have been averted, were it not for a buckboard which careened down the street and stopped in a cloud of dust. Clay took one quick look. Eve was driving it and she never looked more beautiful or more distant and unobtainable. Behind her, on a blanket, was Apache Pat Tanner.

The old coot was almost himself as he sat up, swathed in bandages, and surveyed the bodies of Barton, Gallatin, and Shambrun in the road. He cursed them fluently, then turned his rage on the assembled crowd, telling them what he thought of them for ungrateful pups, after all he'd done for them, and now they'd tied up with a low conniving scoundrel who thought he could break the Big T and drive him off the range.

In the midst of Pat's raving and ranting, Clay spoke up quietly. "Shut up, Pat! You're not in the right any more than these people are."

Pat, caught unawares, opened and closed his mouth like a dying fish. When his breath came back, he roared, "What! Did I hear you aright, Clay? You taking sides against me now and going over to them mangy critters!"

The crowd fell silent, seeing a clash of wills stronger than their own. They parted silently as Clay passed through. He turned and spoke again. His voice was quiet but it carried so he could be heard clearly.

"I'm goin' to tell you all a little story and some of it ain't so nice." His eyes flickered briefly towards the bodies.

Clay stopped for a minute, then turned to George Weaver. "Better let the ranchers out, too, George. I want them to hear what I got to say."

George took one look at Clay's face, then moved hurriedly to obey.

Jim Chalice, followed by the others came out, squinting in the sun. They stood there, waiting; evidently George had told them Clay was outside and wanting to speak his piece.

Clay addressed himself to Chalice, knowing that if he could convince Jim, the other members of the Pool would fall into line.

"I'm sorry it had to happen like this, Jim," Quantrelle said. "But right then you didn't give us much time and it seemed like this was the best way to go about it. I know you got hard feelings — so would I have if I was you — but raidin' a round-up crew is a mean Injun trick and we had to stop you. 'Sides," he continued soberly, "the whole idea was to get you out of the way so's you or the rest of the members of the Pool wouldn't get hurt. Barton, Gallatin, and Shambrun was crooks and we didn't have to be too careful 'bout what happened to them."

Chalice interrupted him with a hard look in his eyes. "Talk's cheap, mister. All we know's that you busted our Pool, gunned down three of our friends, and now you

212

come crawlin' around with weasel words. Maybe you think you won right now, but let me tell you somethin', there ain't a man around these parts, nor a woman neither that don't know what's happened and none of the decent folk'll ever say a word to you agin. Ye're nothin' but a gun-crazy killer hired by old Pat Tanner and if either you or him ever steps foot on my proppity, I'm gonna shoot you down like a wolf."

The crowd gasped, sure that Jim had signed his death warrant. No man could talk to Quantrelle like that and live. Clay's face drained of color and then his eyes caught Eve's face. There was a pleading look there. *You must make him understand, it was saying.*

Clay drew a deep breath and when he spoke, his voice was harsh.

"I don't blame you for what you're thinking. But it ain't all white and black like you and the rest of them here are figurin'. Now that you said what's in your mind, you're gonna hear what I got to tell you. I was in the Lincoln County Wars — I guess you all know that. We thought we was in the right and we fought for it. I ain't ashamed of fightin' and killin' a man fair, but that feudin' taught me something. That was a range war, just like what you got here, and after it

213

was all over, there wasn't anybody you could say was the winner. Everbody lost because we was too thick-headed to understand that when we thought we was in the right, there was always the other guy, and him sure he was right, too! I ain't talkin' for Pat here — I know just what kind of an old hard-bitten rannyhan *he* is — but the rest of you ain't no better. You got a nice town and some mighty nice ranchin' country around here and all o' you start actin' like a bunch of danged fools with itchy trigger fingers."

A voice from the crowd — a woman's voice — suddenly spoke up in support. "Yo're plumb right, Mister! I allus said the menfolk round here were nothin' better than a passel o' kids! Stead o' working and buildin' us up a nice town, they got nothin' better to do than ridin' around nights, shootin' each other!"

Chalice was a fair man, though the hardness had not gone from his voice. "Mebbe what you say is true, Mister, if old Pat here, was willin' to listen to reason and not go lordin' it over us all the time like he owned us. But you still ain't answered why you broke up our Pool and shot down three of our men. I ain't saying I allus agreed with Barton, but he was the only one who was trying to do something for us small ranchers."

Clay nodded. "Yeah, I guess I got to explain that. There's only one thing wrong with the way you said it. Barton wasn't tryin' to do things for you — he was aimin' to do 'em *to* you!" He held up his hand at the storm of protests that swelled through the crowd.

"Now, wait a minute! I ain't just talking for the sound of my voice. Barton was a crook, and if you-all weren't so all-fired hot on fightin' Pat Tanner, you'd have figured it out a long time ago." Quickly and tersely he told them of Barton's nefarious plotting, of how he had mistaken Quantrelle for his hired gunman, how he had boasted of his plans against all the ranchers and how he had used Ike Gallatin as his secret spy at the Big T. When he'd finished, he said:

"There it is. And it ain't a nice picture. Barton had his schemes against the lot of you, and if he wasn't lying there dead now, he'd be figurin' right now how to cheat you."

The whole town looked aghast at the revelation, particularly Jim Chalice and the rancher members of the Pool. Jim seemed a little uncertain, but his eyes were narrow as he threw out one question to Clay.

"If what you say is true, Mister, then we're all bigger fools than God meant to walk around down here. But your just saying it, don't necessarily make it so. You got any proof that Barton was aimin' to do us like you said?"

That was the crucial question that Clay had been awaiting and dreading. No, there was no proof. There were only two men who could confirm it — Gallatin and Shambrun — and they were both lying there in the dust, dead to speak no more.

His hesitation brought Chalice up. His voice was sharp as he repeated his query. "I ast you something, Mister! You gonna tell us —"

A sweet clear voice rang above the heads of the crowd. It was Eve, standing in the buckboard. Clay stared at her wonderingly. How could she have any knowledge —

"Yes, Dad it's true!"

"What do you mean, Eve!" her father demanded.

"I'm telling you it's true," she said. "And I know! After Sheriff Weaver came to arrest you this morning, I drove out to Hal's ranch to tell him what happened." Her face colored, remembering something. "You see, I was blind, too! I believed Hal was working for us all. But when I got to the ranch, I learned something. They didn't hear me ride in, and as I came up the steps of the house, I heard Hal and those other two drinking and laughing. They were talking about their plans and I stopped and heard the whole thing. It's just like Clay said: they were going to use the Pool to drive Pat out and by then all the ranchers would be bankrupt so Hal and his friends would take over the whole Basin! When I heard that, I crept off the porch, got my horse and rode over to the Big T. Pat said he knew all about it, Clay had told him. I was worried about what would happen here when Hal and his friends made the jailbreak, so I hitched up the buckboard and brought Pat in to help."

Her clear eyes looked down on Clay and the message in them was plain for him to read. He moved swiftly through the crowd to the buckboard, held up his hand as she stepped down. They stood there and looked at each other, and then she melted into his arms in the way of a woman with her mate. They were oblivious to everything, to the crowd behind them which surged around the buckboard as Apache Pat Tanner hemmed and hawed and finally thrust out a great paw to Jim Chalice.

"I guess I'm just like Clay says — just an

ornery old galoot that oughta have his britches warmed up." He glanced speculatively down at Clay and Eve, still melted in each other's arms.

" 'Sides, if Clay's gonna be my ramrod, it ain't fittin' for him to be fightin' with his future paw-in-law!"

ABOUT THE AUTHOR

Leslie Ernenwein was born in Oneida, New York. He began his newspaper career as a telegraph editor, but at eighteen went West where he rambled from Montana to Mexico, working as a cowboy and then as a freelance writer. In the mid 1930s he went back East to work for the *Schenectady Sun.* In 1938 he got a reporting position with the *Tucson Daily Citizen* and moved to Tucson permanently. Later that year he began writing Western fiction for pulp magazines, becoming a regular contributor to *Dime Western* and *Star Western.* His first Western novel, *Gunsmoke Galoot,* appeared in 1941, and was quickly followed by *Kinkade of Red Butte* and *Boss of Panamint* in 1942. In addition to publishing novels regularly, Ernenwein continued to contribute heavily to the magazine market, both Western fiction and factual articles. Among his finest work in the 1940s are *Rebels Ride Proudly* (1947)

219

and *Rebel Yell* (1948), both dealing with the dislocations caused by the War Between the States. In the 1950s Ernenwein wrote primarily for original paperback publishers of Western fiction because the pay was better. *High Gun* in 1956, published by Fawcett Gold Medal, won a Spur Award from the Western Writers of America, the first original paperback Western to do so. That same year, since the pulp magazine market had all but vanished, Ernenwein returned to working for the Tucson Daily Citizen, this time as a columnist. Ernenwein's Western fiction may be broadly characterized as moral allegories, light against darkness, and at the center is a protagonist determined to fight against injustice before he is destroyed by it. *Bullet Barricade* (1955), perhaps his most notable novel from the 1950s, best articulates his vision of how the life of man is not governed by a fate over which he has no control, even though life itself may seem like a never-ending contest against moral evil.

We hope you have enjoyed this Large Print book. Other Thorndike, Wheeler, Kennebec, and Chivers Press Large Print books are available at your library or directly from the publishers.

For information about current and upcoming titles, please call or write, without obligation, to:

Publisher
Thorndike Press
295 Kennedy Memorial Drive
Waterville, ME 04901
Tel. (800) 223-1244

or visit our Web site at:

http://gale.cengage.com/thorndike

OR

Chivers Large Print
published by BBC Audiobooks Ltd
St James House, The Square
Lower Bristol Road
Bath BA2 3SB
England
Tel. +44(0) 800 136919
email: bbcaudiobooks@bbc.co.uk
www.bbcaudiobooks.co.uk

All our Large Print titles are designed for easy reading, and all our books are made to last.